Sanitarium Magazine
Issue no. 44

Thank you to all of our contributors, we couldn't have done it without you.

FACULTY MEMBERS

Dr. Sputnik
Dr. Muratori
Dr. Soldan
Dr. Algee
Dr. Marceau
Dr. Warra

Contents

ISSUE FORTY-FOUR

Dear Reader,

Horror writers put up with a lot from other genres writers, we are seen as the black sheep of the writing family. Is it because we play in the sandbox of monsters, gore, torturing poor souls and damming them to hell, or is it because we are open to all notions to scare our reader as the end goal?

Thriller writers play in this sandbox as well but with a human mask upon the killer's face. However, we soldier on and press ahead with our writing and for that I say thank you.

The past couple of months the human side of horror was exposed, which is far scarier than anything within fiction - as this was real life. As a genre and a people, we need to stand together and report anything of this nature as soon as it happens. Even if it stops one predator from attacking a fellow convention attendee this shit stops now.

Sorry for the rant but it had to be said – stay safe.

Barry Skelhorn

Dead Ronnie And I by David A. Riley

I always fancied the idea of spending a couple of years alone on a desert island, with a supply of fruit, some easily caught (and easily cooked) birds and a lagoon or two where I could catch fish. The weather would have to be sunny, apart from the occasional shower to keep me supplied with fresh water. Sunday mornings listening to *Desert Island Discs* had always been a pleasant half hour of daydreams, when I would imagine getting away from the pressures of modern-day life.

I never imagined I would end up on a deserted island with weather less friendly than the radio program conjured up.

It had been a strange year. A hard year. And if ever I fancied an escape of sorts it was then.

Ronnie Martin and I had been running a shipping company in the Hebrides for the past five years. We bought out Angus McBride when he retired. His sons had no interest in the aircraft business and there was no one else for him to leave it to, so he figured he might as well take what money he could get for it and retire. Ronnie and I had been made redundant and had worked together most of our adult lives. We had started at the same company within months of each other, married only months apart – and got divorced around the same time too and for much the same reasons. I know, the usual problem with travelling salesmen, playing around. Not much of a surprise, I suppose. So, when we ended up with a decent payout, it seemed only natural we should pool resources and go into business together. I already had a flying licence. A few more lessons got my licence upgraded so I could fly McBride's de Haviland amphibious seaplane, which he'd used for the less accessible islands where the only landing strips were stretches of beach or a sheltered bay.

It was late autumn when things went wrong. The weather had been bad for the past few days. Our next shipment to Spring Isle, an isolated community of a few hundred souls, was overdue. We had delayed setting out till the storms swept past, knowing it wouldn't be possible to land in the island's harbour while they were blowing. On top of all this the national news was worrying. There had been outbreaks of senseless violence across the UK and the rest of the world, rising to epidemic proportions. What had at first been riots had become even worse, with wild rumours flying around, especially after governments declared Martial Law across the globe. Television had been reduced to one channel that showed reruns of old shows with a heavily censored news broadcast every hour.

There were reports of unrest in towns and villages as far north as our base in Scotland.

"I don't like the sound of it," Ronnie said after we watched the latest broadcast. It had been short, terse - and worryingly uninformative.

"Stay put and stay calm," I paraphrased. "Not reassuring." We were in our office at the airfield. Rain lashed the windows, though we could still see our plane through the open doors of the hangar. It was fully fuelled, ready for take-off at a break in the weather.

"I wouldn't mind getting away to Spring Isle till the troubles are over."

There'd been talk of tens, maybe hundreds of thousands being killed in the violence – and weirder stuff too. Stuff neither of us credited, though that didn't stop people talking about it. As if dead men could get up and walk!

"Anyone bitten by the infected should be isolated and kept in secure conditions."

That was one bit of advice we'd heard on the news, though we'd heard those infected – getting bitten or scratched, it seemed, was enough for that to happen – were being shot by police and the army. It was too incredible, and neither of us really believed it. This was Britain, after all. We didn't go round shooting people. This wasn't Bosnia or the Sudan or Syria.

In the distance flames flared across the nearest town. Smoke filled the sky, darker than the clouds.

I shivered.

"If the wind eases a few more knots I'm for going," I said. Ronnie nodded his head. His grey hair looked more silvery now. I wondered if worry was having the same effect on mine. Though we felt safe enough here, no amount of cynicism over the reliability of what we were told on the news could stop us from feeling alarmed.

It was mid-afternoon when the wind dropped and strips of blue appeared through the clouds. It couldn't have happened soon enough. Already smoke was streaming from a housing estate a mile away from us. Now and then, through the wind, I could swear there were screams, sometimes gunfire. Whatever was happening was getting close.

Too close.

We climbed in the airplane and I started its rotor. I radioed the watch tower but there was only silence. I looked back at Ronnie, sat behind me.

"Bugger clearance. If they've gone, fuck 'em." Ronnie grinned. There was fear in his eyes for all his bravado. It was then that we saw them. It was the biggest mob I'd seen in my life. I hadn't even known there were so many people hereabouts. They came on in an endless wave that crushed the perimeter fence as if it was made out of string.

"Get moving," Ronnie said.

I didn't need urging. Increasing the power to the engine I steered us through the hangar doors onto the airfield. A brisk wind was blowing but nothing we couldn't cope with as I accelerated down the runway. It was then the mob surged towards us as if drawn by the noise of the engine. I looked back at Ronnie.

"Don't mind if you crack a few heads," he called over the roar of the powerful Pratt and Whitney engine. "Let's get moving."

Which was easier said than done. Some of the rioters had reached the side of the plane and were hammering it with their fists. We were still only moving at a walking pace and I was worried that some of them would make a grab at the tail plane and damage it.

There was a sudden increase in sound and I realised that someone had managed to get hold of the handle outside and dragged the door to the luggage compartment open.

"Get it shut," I told Ronnie. "We can't take off like this." Ronnie hefted a monkey wrench. "Leave it to me," he said. "I'll sort the fuckers."

I saw that one of them had managed to drag himself inside the hold. The shock of seeing him made me swing the de Haviland off course towards the grass. None of the TV broadcasts had shown the rioters close up and had only hinted about the effects of their infection. It was only now that realised it was worse than I had imagined. The man's face was a disgusting mess of torn flesh and exposed gristle. One eye had been torn from its socket. The other stared with such intense hatred I felt a shiver run down my spine. Ronnie swung the monkey wrench at him, crushing his skull, then pushed his body back into the others who had managed to drag themselves onboard. Wielding the wrench like a cudgel, Ronnie killed another of the boarders, then battered the last of them back towards the door. Again and again, he pummelled him. The man grabbed Ronnie's arm, before a final blow sent him tumbling out onto the runway as I managed to accelerate away from the mob. Ronnie slammed the door shut, blotting them from sight.

After that we took off. Within minutes we were flying out across the sea, my hands trembling on the joystick as I stared at the waves below us.

Ronnie lurched onto the seat beside me. His face was ashen.

"One of the fuckers got me." He showed me his arm. Ragged lines had been gouged into it. They were bleeding badly.

"There's a doctor on Spring Isle. She'll fix you up."

"I'll need antibiotics. God knows what germs were under the bastard's nails. Did you see the state of him?"

I wondered if I looked as shocked as Ronnie. "Like a living corpse." I shook my head, unable to understand what had happened.

"What the hell is wrong with them?" Ronnie asked.

The wind was against us, slowing us down, and what should have been a two-hour flight was going to take longer. Having to concentrate on dealing with the weather, I had little time to talk and Ronnie eventually grew silent too, sitting back in his seat, exhausted after the fight at the airfield. The weather worsened steadily and I was not looking forward to landing at Spring Isle. I knew it would probably take all the skill I had to get us down in one piece.

We were still several miles from our destination when Ronnie started to moan. For the first time in over an hour I looked at him and was alarmed how ill he was. His face was grey; perspiration dripped from him as if he was running a fever. Had the scratches become septic so quickly? Or was it that disease the news had been babbling about for days?

Glancing at the clock I realised it would be at least twenty minutes before we reached our destination, though the doctor's clinic was close to the harbour. Ronnie looked so ill, though, I was scared he would die before we got there.

"Hang on," I said to him, though I don't think he heard me as I peered through the windscreen, trying to see through the rain lashing across it.

Several small islands passed beneath us and I knew it wouldn't be long before I would see our destination. Then Ronnie, climbing to his feet, lashed at me. Caught off guard, I was dazed by the blow and immediately the plane rolled on its side as my hands flew from the joystick to fend him off. Overbalanced, Ronnie crashed against the panels, which gave me time to clear my head and try to restore the plane's flight. I glanced at Ronnie as we levelled out. There was a look on his face that warned me the fight wasn't over with yet. He lurched towards me, impeded by the cramped confines of the cabin. Ready this time, I hit him in the face. It should have stunned him but it didn't seem to bother him at all. His fingers grabbed for my throat, gripping like claws. I hit him again, then grasped his wrists to pull him from me. Though his face was full of rage, he seemed to lack the strength to harm me as badly as he wanted to do, as if he was moving in his sleep. Even so, with fifteen stones of weight behind him, I had to struggle to fend him off. Again I lost control of the plane. Its nose dipped and there was a horrible, terrifying screech as air streamed across its wings. We had gone into a dive.

"Ronnie! You'll kill us both!" I was shouting to deaf ears. I half turned from him, made a grab with one hand for the joystick and pulled it back as best I could but it wasn't enough. It could never be enough. We were hurtling too fast. I needed both hands to pull us free but I couldn't do that while Ronnie was trying to grasp my throat.

The next few minutes are hazy in my memory. I must have blacked out when we hit the sea because the next thing I remember were ice cold waves rushing over me, covering my head. My ears were filled with a roaring sound and I could barely see. Sparks flared, and I became aware of the pale greyness outside as the plane tilted on the sea. Somehow, we had managed to land intact but I knew we were sinking. Water surged through rifts. Already it had reached my knees. I turned round but Ronnie was nowhere in sight. Realising that I had to think of my own safety first I struggled towards the door, grabbing a lifejacket on my way and somehow managing to strap it on. Seconds later I tugged the door open and the sea flooded in. Inflating my lifejacket, though, I lunged out before the plane sank beneath the waves.

The rest was chaos. In those first few minutes in the sea, I was sure I would be killed by hypothermia. I had never been so cold in my life. Sea water covered my head time and again as I swam away from the sinking plane, with no idea where the nearest land was or how far away it might be. Several times I blacked out, only the lifejacket keeping me afloat. Jostled by the waves, I regained consciousness long enough to kick my legs to propel me forwards, though whether I was moving out to sea or towards whatever land there was hereabouts I had no idea. Blind faith was all I had left – that and the will to survive.

I seemed to have been battling the waves for days, though it could not have been much more than an hour when I finally felt land beneath my feet. A rock grazed my shin, making me clench my eyes against the pain as I wallowed forwards onto an abrasive mix of shells and boulders. Dully, somewhere inside my head, I realised I had reached land and, with an effort, my clothes so sodden they weighed me down, I managed to totter forwards, tripping over more rocks and picking myself up till the water was shallow enough for me to stand upright. I strained my eyes in the murky twilight to make out where I was, shivering, but it was growing dark fast and all I could see was a long, low silhouette of ground, black against the skyline. I staggered up what passed for a beach to find some shelter of sorts in a deep crevice between the rocks. I was deathly cold but at least I could rest. I was so tired all I wanted was sleep.

How long I slept I have no idea. The next thing I realised it was dawn. A dim light shone through an endless stretch of dull grey clouds, with only a tinge of red to indicate the sun. Still damp, my clothes were drier than when I collapsed into the cleft and, as I rubbed my hands together to restore some sort of circulation, I forced myself to explore where I was. I hoped I would find I was on Spring Isle but I soon realised I had had no such luck. The land rose to a low hill perhaps a hundred feet high. I clambered up its slopes, sparsely covered in grass, with a few thorny shrubs spread across it. It took me less than half an hour to reach the summit, from where I could see the whole island. Some desert paradise! Trust my luck to end up on a windswept mound of barren rocks.

It was the grimmest, dreariest stretch of land I had seen in my life. The best I could say about it was that there was fresh water of sorts, small pools scarcely bigger than my cupped hands scattered amongst the rocks, too high to be contaminated by the sea. But what was there to eat? I wouldn't last long off the coarse, scraggly clumps of grass! And there didn't seem any other form of wildlife here than a few seagulls, and I had no hope of catching one of them. Even if I did there was nothing to cook it with other than the thorn bushes. And being a non-smoker, I didn't even have matches or a lighter.

I stared across the sea, hoping to see another island that might be a better refuge if I could only get to it, but visibility was poor and I couldn't make anything out beyond a few hundred yards.

Feeling hungrier as the morning went on; I strolled around the shoreline, looking for anything that might be edible, though I was not optimistic. There are probably people who could have made a feast out of the shell fish, shrimps and other creatures that lived in the rock pools and the patches of coarse sand that were scattered around the island, but I had no idea what to do with any of them – nor hungry enough yet to try.

Some debris from the seaplane had washed ashore, but there was little I could make use of other than a few sticks of wood that might make a fire if I could figure out how to get one started. There was a package addressed to someone on Spring Isle, battered and waterlogged. Inside what was left of the brown paper and soggy cardboard I found a fruitcake wrapped in cellophane and an unbroken bottle of sherry, a birthday present from someone's aunt. Clutching these to my chest I took them uphill to the best shelter I could find and set about eating some of the cake, carefully rewrapping the rest of it and putting it in one of the pockets of my coat for later. A few sips of sherry were enough to give me a feeling of warmth that helped me relax. I knew I was not out of danger yet, that the cold or starvation might do me in within the next few weeks if I couldn't get off this island and find somewhere better, but for now I had food and something to drink besides the pools of rainwater - and a brief respite.

Needing to keep moving as much as I could to stay warm - or as warm as I could get – I spent most of the day beach combing. I was sure something new was always being washed up on shore. By late afternoon I managed to find some plastic bottles which I filled with water from the rock pools in case the rain stopped and the pools dried up. A length of wood that had probably been part of a fence somewhere gave me a walking stick and something to poke into dodgier looking lumps of debris. Then I saw one of the de Haviland's floats. It wasn't in good condition, with tears where the struts that once held it to the aircraft's body had snapped when we crashed, but it still looked buoyant. The wind and tide had washed it up on a ridge of low rocks several feet from the sea. I gave it a push and, though it was heavy, I managed to move it several inches. Bit by bit it would not take me long to get it back into the water. If I lay on top of its flat surface, I should be able to use it to carry me off this island. Whatever happened, it would be better than staying stuck here to face inevitable starvation or freezing to death when winter set in.

For the next hour I inched the float nearer the sea. It was exhausting and I frequently had to take a rest but at least the exertion helped warm me up! In a surprisingly short time, I managed to inch the float to the edge of the waves. It was then I noticed something bobbing in the water out to sea. I strained my eyes against the sunlight that shimmered across the waves to try and make out what the object was, wondering if it might be something useful, till I realised it was a head.

A human head.

Startled, I jumped away from the float. The head was coming nearer, as its neck and shoulders and the rest of its torso emerged from the water. It was the face that alarmed me. It was Ronnie's. Unmistakably Ronnie's. Except Ronnie's skin had never looked so white or so shiny, as if it was layered with wet soap. His hair hung in sodden locks, though there were bare patches of bony whiteness on top of his head where it had fallen away. But it was Ronnie's eyes and gaping jaws that scared me the most. His eyes were dead, unfocussed, but they could see. They moved in their sockets, turning in my direction. Then his jaws, gaping in the sea water as if it didn't bother him, began to move as if they were chewing.

I retreated from the float as Ronnie lurched out of the seawater onto the beach. Water streamed from his clothes as he stepped towards me. Even more quickly I stepped away from him, wary of tripping on the stones behind me.

"What do you want, Ronnie?"

Even as I spoke, I knew I was wasting my time. Whatever was going on inside Ronnie's head it wasn't remotely like cogent thinking. There was no intelligence in his mottled face, just rage. This wasn't Ronnie anymore. The man I'd known for so many years had gone. This thing was an abomination.

I retreated along the beach. As I did so the creature staggered towards me, its pace so slow I was soon out of sight of it. But whether it could see me or not seemed to make no difference.

It still came after me. I could hear the clattering of the stones it stumbled over. Sometimes it fell, but that didn't seem to bother it either. Whether it grazed itself or not, it pulled itself to its feet once more and continued its pursuit.

I hurried round the island till I reached the float and started to push it towards the sea, but the tide was on its way out and the gap had grown. Again and again, I put everything I had into budging the float, till I heard Ronnie's feet. Letting go, I ran as fast as I dared over the rocks and pebbles around the island, Ronnie relentlessly following me. Time and again I returned to the float, pushing it out a few feet further towards the sea before Ronnie's reappearance forced me to stop.

Eventually I got it to the edge of the waves but Ronnie was again behind me and I had to make a break for it. This time I ran faster. I didn't want the tide to widen the gap yet again. I needed only a few minutes and I knew I could be away from here and away from that thing that had once been my friend.

Everything was spinning by the time I reached the float once more; I was so exhausted. But I didn't have time to relax. Ronnie was only minutes behind me. I heaved against the float, feeling its buoyancy as the outgoing tide suddenly dragged it forwards. Now it was my turn to race alongside the float. I lunged on top of it, grasping whatever remained of the broken struts to drag myself up as a wave pulled us away from the beach. I clung on with all my strength.

The wind was blowing away from the island, which helped to speed us along. I looked back as the island fell away behind me. Ronnie had reached the edge of the beach, staring at me. He clumped forward step by step into the waves. Deeper and deeper he lurched till they rose about his chest. Even then he kept going. A moment later the sea swept across his face, submerging him beneath it. I shuddered, imagining his cold body dragging itself through the depths beneath me.

After that I had no time for anything but to concentrate on staying on top of the float as it pitched this way then that on the sea. Every moment it was in danger of overturning and plunging me into the ice-cold water, but somehow, I managed to keep it upright, even though my hands were soon so numb I could no longer feel them.

Often during that night, I felt sure I was going to die. Just as often I even wished I could die. The fear and pain and intense cold were combining to sap what will to live I still had left. Then the sounds around me changed. I heard the rush of waves hitting something hard. I looked up and ahead of me there was a break in the skyline, a dark mass that had to be land.

I was found by some local fishermen. I was delirious by then, out of my mind with exhaustion and hypothermia. From what I was told later I was close to death. They took me to the doctor's surgery in Spring Isle's harbour. Twenty-four hours later I was asked to explain what had happened, which I did as well as I could.

Though Spring Isle is free from whatever has infected most of the rest of the world, everyone on the island knew about it from TV.

A delegation of the island's council came to see me when I was fit enough to get out of bed.

"We're free from the infection and intend to stay that way," Ian McCloud, leader of the island's council, informed me. I'd known him for years and respected his integrity. I could tell he was not happy about what he had to say to me.

"I'm free from it too," I assured him.

The island's doctor, Alice McRae agreed. "Apart from the effects of exposure you're as fit as a fiddle."

"Ronnie Martin was infected, though," McCloud said. "And from what you've told us he's following you."

"Seems to be," I admitted. Which is when it hit me. The half dozen people who had come to see me, all of them leading members of the island community, were scared of what had happened elsewhere happening here as well.

"We can't risk him coming to Spring Isle," McCloud said. "While you're with us he's likely to find his way here. He could arrive anywhere along the coastline."

"And attack anyone he met," Alice added. "Which is how the infection would start."

Which is why I'm back on that desolate lump of rock, ferried on one of Spring Isle's fishing boats.

"When your friend is dead you can come back to us. While he's out there looking for you, he's too dangerous."

The cold logic was inarguable. This time, though, I am armed. The islanders have given me a fully loaded rifle, a sleeping bag, a one-man tent and a supply of food and water. They'll return for me in a week's time. By then it's expected that poor dead Ronnie will have met his fate.

Now I'm sat here, waiting. It's cold and dark and I can hear the sea surging all around and the non-stop wailing of the wind, while somewhere in the depths of the sea I can imagine Ronnie trudging my way, guided by whatever blind instinct motivates his body.

I hope he gets here soon.

The End.

CASE #77902

DEAD RONNIE AND I
BY DAVID A. RILEY

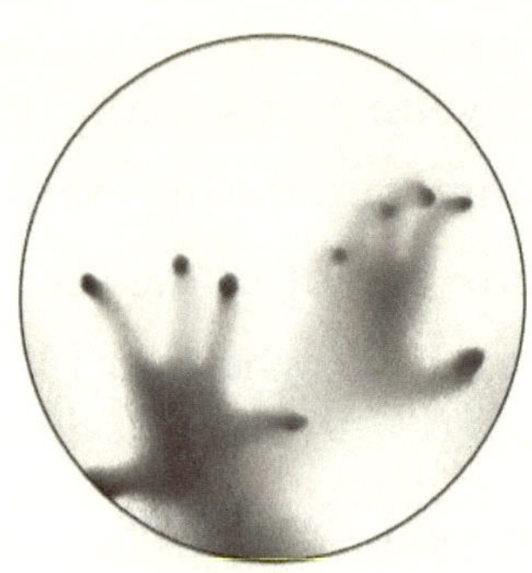

David A. Riley writes horror, fantasy and SF stories.

In 1995, along with his wife, Linden, he edited and published a fantasy/SF magazine, Beyond.

His first professionally published story was in the 11th Pan Book of Horror in 1970. This was reprinted in 2012 in The Century's Best Horror Fiction edited by John Pelan for Cemetery Dance. He has had numerous stories published by Doubleday, DAW, Corgi, Sphere, Roc, Playboy Paperbacks, Robinsons, etc., and in magazines such as Aboriginal Science Fiction, Dark Discoveries, Fear, Whispers, and Fantasy Tales. His first collection of stories (4 long stories and a novelette) was published by Hazardous Press in 2012, His Own Mad Demons.

A Lovecraftian novel, The Return, was published by Blood BoundBooks in the States in 2013.

A second collection of his stories, all of which were professionally published prior to 2000, The Lurkers in the Abyss & Other Tales of Terror, was launched at the World Fantasy Convention in 2013 by Shadow Publishing. Hazardous Press published his third short story collection, Their Cramped Dark World and Other Tales, in 2015. Both Hazardous Press collections have now been reprinted, with brand new covers, by Parallel Universe Publications.

A fantasy novel, Goblin Mire, and a horror novel, Moloch's Children, were both published in 2015.

He and his wife recently relaunched Parallel Universe Publications, which originally published Beyond. Parallel Universe published twelve books in 2015, including an anthology of new stories, Kitchen Sink Gothic, edited by David A. Riley and Linden Riley. David Riley's stories have been translated into Italian, German, Spanish and Russian.

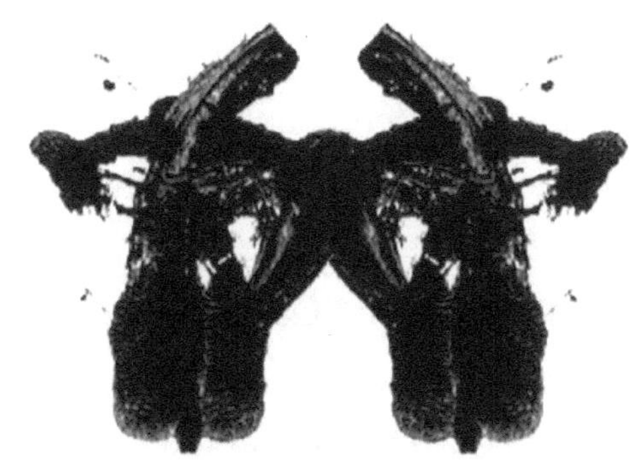

Pruritus by Trevor Neil White

Every year, the united states government files an average of 90,000 criminal cases in the federal courts. In a majority, defendants accept a plea bargain or settlement, sparing judges from a deluge of arguments over relatively minor offenses.

However, among these "terminated" proceedings, a microscopic minority is never formally assigned to a docket — no scholarly database will report it, no judicial archive or annual statistics will acknowledge it. The reasons are largely mundane, from clerical error to sheer brevity of litigation, but some determinants exist at the system's shadowy fringes: powerful figures extinguishing what little light touches their transgressions, or justice implicating state secrets passed under cover of plausible deniability.

And then there are cases like *State v. Eckbaum.*

At 11:05 PM EST on March 29, 2013, Emergency Services in Manhattan, New York received a call from the cellphone of William Eckbaum, age eighteen. Eckbaum, crying and out of breath, provided directions to an apartment on the Upper East Side and hung up. Officers and paramedics arrived at 11:20 PM, where they found the bodies of Carla Epps, age nineteen, and Anthony Cutler, age eighteen (the decedents), in a bedroom with its door open and lights on. The decedents wore only underwear and lay flat in pools of blood (Epps parallel on the bed, Cutler on the floor). Their skin was covered in dozens of two- to three-inch narrow slashes with gashes one-third of an inch wide at an end.

The premises showed no signs of forced entry. Among neighbors questioned later, several on the adjacent floors indicated that a young man consistent with Eckbaum's description had knocked on their doors the previous evening to say he would be shooting a "stunt" video the next day and that, as one recalled, "[he'd] try to keep it down, but if you hear any shouting, screaming, whatever, don't panic."

An eight-inch stainless steel kitchen knife bearing Eckbaum's fingerprints lay in the blood near the bodies, while a Panasonic v250 camcorder covered in the same fingerprints was retrieved from beneath the radiator against the northern wall. The camcorder was damaged such that the internal screen was shattered and its Micro SD card slot bent shut, preventing access to footage inside until authorities could secure proper technical support several weeks into the investigation. A camera tripod stood in the kitchen, while the decedents' clothes lay in a pile behind Eckbaum's bed.

Officers traced Eckbaum's cellphone to a convenience store's alley eight blocks northeast, after two return calls went unanswered. Although he enthusiastically accompanied authorities, he became hostile when questioned, especially upon learning that a sweep of his apartment turned up no "bugs." He repeatedly requested that his building be evacuated and unsuccessfully attempted to flee the precinct. When the aforementioned evidence was processed, officers placed him under arrest on suspicion of a double homicide. Eckbaum's parents, Joseph and Naomi Eckbaum, were subsequently notified, and remained cooperative throughout the proceedings.

Eckbaum received legal counsel from his parents' attorney, Chris Alvarez. In a motion to dismiss, Alvarez argued that the charges were based purely on circumstantial and inconclusive forensic evidence, and forwarded that Cutler had committed murder-suicide under the influence of illegal substances.

In preparation for trial before the Supreme Court of New York, the defense produced three Exhibits:

#1 - Audio Recording of Eckbaum's 911 Call [Transcript]

Dispatcher: 911, what is your emergency?

Eckbaum: [Sobbing] They're bleeding! There's things everywhere, it's... oh God, it's all my fault...

Dispatcher: Sir, who's bleeding?

Eckbaum: My friends, Ant[hony], Carla, they're in my room,

I'm on the street, I'm...

Dispatcher: Two people are bleeding?

Eckbaum: Yes! Please, please help!

Dispatcher: Where are they bleeding from?

Eckbaum: Everywhere! It was coming out of their chests and faces and legs and... Jesus, they're dead. [Heavy breathing] Sorry, got to... I'm running. Have... to get out of here, they'll get me.

Dispatcher: Sir, who is "they"? Is somebody else in the building?

Eckbaum: Something! Some *things*! Big [unintelligible] ...they made this noise, and, and crawling everywhere, it was like... [unintelligible; Eckbaum claimed to have run under a bridge at this point]

Dispatcher: Sir, if you're not in any immediate danger, I need you stay where you are, otherwise it'll be difficult for us to—

Eckbaum: It's ███████ off Third Avenue, number 407. Tell their parents I'm so sorry... I can't go back up there.

#2 - Eckbaum's Deposition [Video and Textual Transcript]

THE VIDEOGRAPHER: We are now on record in the matter of State versus Eckbaum, criminal case in the Supreme Court for the State of New York,

Case No. ███████ Today's date is July the 13th, 2013, and the time is approximately 2:00 PM. This video deposition of William A. Eckbaum is being taken at the office of Attorney Chris S. Alvarez, New York. My name is Caroline Strauss. I am the videographer. At this time, would the attorneys please identify themselves and the party they represent, beginning with the party noticing the proceedings.

***

[Eckbaum's deposition spanned over fifty pages; the most relevant excerpts follow.]

EXAMINATION BY ELLEN DERMOT FOR THE STATE

Q: Good afternoon, William.

A: Yeah. Good afternoon.

Q: Is this your first time having your deposition taken?

A: Yes.

Q: So, now, you understand that you have sworn to tell the truth, the whole truth, and nothing but the truth?

A: Yes.

[Eckbaum wears a plain white t-shirt and khakis. He continually scratches himself throughout and has thin scars and reddened skin over most of his neck, face, and forearms. A physical examination, requested by the State, confirmed that these abrasions—as well as others covering his torso, limbs, and upper back—were self-inflicted, the result of extensive scratching.]

***

Q: Tell me a bit about your school.

A: Well, uh, I went to The Dalton School—it's a private college prep place. So for undergrad, I was applying all over the city. Hoped to get into Columbia, study engineering, but... yeah.

Q: Did you receive any acceptance or rejection letters from any universities to which you'd applied?

A: Not then, no, I'd barely started. Just all rejections now, though. Must've heard about all this.

Q: Okay. Tell me a bit about your employment history.

A: I worked part-time at the Best Buy off Lexington and 86th last summer, did some volunteer work during the school year at the homeless shelter 'round there, and... that's about it.

Q: Were you working at the time the deaths occurred?

A: I... no. I was just finishing my senior year.

Q: So, are your parents your main source of money?

A: Yes.

Q: How often do you see your parents?

A: Pretty often, now. But back then, just like once or twice a month. They were working a lot.

Q: How would you describe your relationship with your parents around the time the deaths occurred?

A: We got along fine, still do, under the circumstances. I do love them, if that's what you're wondering. And I owe them a lot—if my dad didn't close deals like he does, I could never dream of an apartment like I've got. Had. Whatever.

Q: And your friends, Anthony and Carla, how long had you known them?

A: I knew Anthony since freshman year of high school, and we started hanging out with Carla junior year.

Q: And how would you describe your relationship with them?

A: Best friends. The 'share a lunch table together and see each-other every weekend' kind.

Q: Would you say that you and Carla were ever romantically involved?

Alvarez: Objection. Will, you don't have to answer that.

A: No. We, I guess, tried something for a while, and it didn't work. But she was cool about it. She said there was always... there would always be another lazy afternoon. [Eckbaum covers his mouth. His shoulders buck.]

Q: Were Carla and Anthony ever romantically involved?

A: [Eckbaum closes his eyes.] No. Next question.

[A prior search authorized for Eckbaum's and Epps' Facebook account private messages and posts confirmed that the pair had casually dated for three weeks in January 2013, although neither the tone nor content of either suggested animosity between the two afterward. A similar search of Cutler's Facebook account was inconclusive.]

***

Q: Have you ever had any medical condition, or been on any kind of medication, that you believe would affect or impact your judgment or memory?

A: I took Tylenol now and then, just for headaches, and... caffeine? Starbucks, Red Bull, Monster, stuff like that. Was on Adderall for a couple months, but that was in middle school.

Q: I'll repeat the question. Do you believe those would affect or impact your judgment or memory?

A: No, I don't 'believe' they would.

Q: Okay. Did you have access to video editing or manipulation software while working on the "FactBlasters" series?

A: Yes, I've got the Adobe Suite and iMovie on my Mac. I'm no expert, though. I can do backgrounds and some basic overlay effects, and that's about it.

Q: Can you remember the last time you inserted or removed the memory card from that camcorder?

A: Yeah, I just stuck it in there, maybe, half an hour before filming.

Q: Did you ever take the memory card out, or rewind or modify the recording in any way?

A: No, never. That was just the... the raw footage.

Q: Did you throw that camera on the ground before leaving your apartment?

A: Yes. I know I should've held on to it, but I... panicked. I had it on me, so I threw it.

Q: What did you do with the knife that was also found by the two bodies?

Alvarez: Objection.

Q: [Clears throat] Do you know how that knife came to be found near the bodies?

A: Yes, I threw it—also threw that. I guess that's out of frame, on the video. I didn't think it'd do anything, though—I mean, not crush something, I guess. But like I said, it was just... panic. Impulse.

Q: What were you doing with the knife prior to moving toward the bedroom?

A: Making a sandwich. [Scoffs] You... you saw the video, right? [To Alvarez] Did she see it? You did.

***

#3 - The Final Video in Eckbaum's Camcorder – March 29, 2013 [Transcript]

The MPEG4 video file transcribed below appears to have been filmed as an intended installment in a YouTube channel series titled "FactBlasters," posted at www.youtube.com/factblasters from August 17, 2012 to March 25, 2013 from Eckbaum's ISP address. The channel and all comments, hyperlinks, and metadata therefrom were removed from YouTube at some point between March 31, 2013 and April 2, 2013 for violating YouTube's terms of service, although the company's legal team could later find no record of the complaint filed. The page currently displays only a "404" error message.

However, a search warrant executed for Eckbaum's personal computer turned up copies of previous episodes, and several witnesses had saved past versions of the channel's pages. The channel's description read "Two geek guys, one geek girl, and a million geek's [sic] questions. Tune in every Friday as we put science to the test and trash the rest!" The series took the form of short "episodes" (ten to twelve minutes) filmed in and around Eckbaum's or the decedents' apartments. The episodes centered on educational skits and experiments performed by Eckbaum, Epps, and Cutler, in which they would "blast" (debunk or clarify) popular assumptions or misconceptions involving chemistry, anatomy, and natural phenomena. The scenes were generally accentuated with humor and stylistic overlays added with film-editing software.

Previous entries included "*Can* You Sneeze With Your Eyes Open?," "3 *Cool* Cures for an Ice Cream Headache," and "Microwave *This*!" The channel had only several hundred subscribers, mostly friends and family of Eckbaum, Epps, and Cutler within New York City.

10:30 AM: [A white male wearing a light blue polo shirt is visible from the chest down. He steps back, revealing himself to be Eckbaum. Behind him is a polished wooden table and three chairs. The table has several short stacks of paper, books, and chemistry
supplies upon it, and behind that is a large "green screen" (the space was later identified as a stretch of blank wall in Eckbaum's living room). He sits at the table and folds his hands.]

Eckbaum: [To the right] Alright!

[Two other people enter the frame: a young woman with cropped blond hair and black-rimmed glasses in a bright red t-shirt (identified as Carla Epps) and a young man with uncombed black hair and a short goatee in a dark green t-shirt (identified as Anthony Cutler). They sit next to Eckbaum.]

Epps: [To Eckbaum] We good?

Eckbaum: We're good.

Cutler: Let's do this!

Epps: Hello, interwebs!

Cutler: And welcome to...

Eckbaum: FactBlasters, the show where we put science to the test and trash the rest! And you know, over the last dozen episodes...
[Epps and Cutler mime scratching their heads in thought.] You've suggested a lot of real head-scratchers for us to run through those tests, so we figured we'd give everybody a little break and do something that requires no scratching at all! Therefore, today's fact is... "Why You Don't Need to Itch!"

[Eckbaum pauses to make several broad hand gestures intermittently throughout this and following scenes; these purportedly represent moments where he intended to insert text or other special effects.]

Eckbaum: How was that?
Cutler: Works for me, man.

[Epps nods and makes an "OK" gesture.]

Eckbaum: Sweet!

[Eckbaum gets up and approaches the camera.]

10:37 AM: [The camera faces Eckbaum at eye level, standing beside a curtained window, in front of a TV set by a pair of bookshelves. He points at the blank space to his side.]

Eckbaum: The "fact," people say, is that an itch is an automatic reaction to dozens of external and internal stimuli, one which satisfies the brain's pleasure center when scratched.

[The camera, apparently on a tripod, quickly pans 90 degrees to Epps sitting in a recliner, legs crossed.]

Epps: But the truth is, itching is a vestigial bodily function, like sweaty palms or carsickness. Oh, sure, there are "legitimate" reasons for itching—like chicken pox, bug bites, and some spinal disorders—but most of the time, our beautifully complicated human brain is just getting its wires crossed, and it overreacts to nothing at all!

[The camera pans once more to Cutler at close range.]

Cutler: And as far as the nervous system cares, the signals for itchiness are those for pain—but while pain indicates that the body's in danger, the discomfort from an itch itself is totally psychological. Still, it's estimated that the average person itches themselves hundreds of times a day, sometimes just from the thought of being itchy.

[The camera pans 180 degrees back around to Eckbaum.]

Eckbaum: Therefore, on today's episode of FactBlasters, Anthony and Carla are going to take on a challenge we believe is unprecedented: Not itch themselves for twelve hours straight!

10:43 AM: [The camera faces Eckbaum from above, to his left. Part of the kitchen's Formica countertop is visible behind him.]

Eckbaum: Now, we recognize that it's impossible to completely stop itching yourself for that long—the friction of your feet on the floor or your limbs moving against each-other will sort of constitute a 'scratch.' So, if it helps, think of it more as "itch yourself as little as possible for twelve hours!"

Cutler: [Off-camera] Oh yeah, that makes our goal very clear.

Epps: [Off-camera] Um, guys, I think we should cut that part out.

Eckbaum: Yeah, I know, but we gotta acknowledge it or the comments section will never let up.

10:45 AM: [The camera is focused on a hundred-dollar bill sticking out of a wallet held above a carpeted floor]

Eckbaum: And just to sweeten the deal, whoever lasts longest will win this sweet cash right here!

Cutler: [Off-camera] And Chipotle for a month!
Eckbaum: That, too.

10:59 AM: [Eckbaum is sitting on a couch with an iPhone in his hand; the "Clock" app is open. Cutler is to his right and then Epps, leaning toward the camera.]

Epps: We know even the Internet doesn't want to watch twelve hours of two people not scratching themselves, so Will is going to film in quick bits over that time and string it together, m'kay?

Eckbaum: That means we'll be running on the honor policy! So, fifteen seconds until 11:00 AM, Eastern Standard Time... anything you want to get ready before we begin?

Cutler: Bare feet, light 'n loose-fitting shirt and shorts—I'm good.

Epps: Me too.

Eckbaum: Alright... five, four, three, two... Go!

[Cutler scratches his armpit like an ape.]

Eckbaum: [Laughs] Alright, let's start over!

11:02 AM: [Eckbaum lounges next to Epps and Cutler, who are sitting with their legs slightly apart and hands gently resting by their thighs. The scene is otherwise identical.]

Eckbaum: [Looking at his phone.] Alright... go!

[Cutler and Epps remain motionless for five seconds. Cutler twitches slightly.]

Cutler: Oh, there's the first one. Left eyebrow.

Epps: Dang it, you made me think of it. Now I've got that and my toe.

Cutler: Argh! [He contorts his face, smiling] New pact: we don't mention it out loud, 'kay?

Eckbaum: [Laughs] I'll be right back.

11:33 AM: [Eckbaum is filming himself at arm's length. The living room is visible behind him.]

Eckbaum: Okay, it's been half an hour now that Anthony and Carla are itch-free! Let's check in...

[Camera follows Eckbaum into the living room, where Cutler and Epps stand in front of the TV swiveling in place making jerking motions.]

Eckbaum: How's it going, guys?

Epps: It's everywhere! I didn't—ah, ooh—even know I still had this much leg hair to tangle. That's some of it, right? Tangled hairs? [She flinches her foot.] Ah, that one actually stung a little.

Eckbaum: How about you, Anthony, any stinging?

Cutler: [Balancing on one foot] Oh, y'know, here and there.

Eckbaum: Well, I bet you could use a distraction... I know! Let's watch a movie! [Eckbaum produces a DVD copy of "Star Wars Episode V" from somewhere below the frame.]

11:43 AM: [The camera tightly focuses on the TV, as the opening crawl of the film scrolls and the main theme blares though the speakers.]

Eckbaum: [Off-screen] I'll go make lunch. Ant, you want grilled cheese?

1:05 PM: [The camera angles down at the TV and couch, where Epps and Cutler sit fidgeting.]

Eckbaum: Status report, guys?

Cutler: [Points at screen] Well, I'm feeling pretty envious of Luke's ex-hand. What's a lightsaber go for these days?

Eckbaum: [Laughs] Does it still sting?

Cutler: Earlier, yeah, but.. nah, it's funny, it's kinda just a, a...
dull hum now, y'know? Maybe I'm gettin' a second wind.

Eckbaum: Ah, Carla, no shimmying!

Epps: [Stands up from the couch] I'm gonna go jog around the block.

Eckbaum: Nope, gotta stick to the apartment.

Epps: [Dragged-out] No fun...

Eckbaum: I know—board games next!

2:15 PM: [The camera is at ground level. The coffee table previously in front of the couch is gone, replaced with the board and pieces for "Monopoly." Cutler and Epps rest on their haunches, while Eckbaum, sitting cross-legged facing the camera, rolls the dice.]

Eckbaum: Community Chest!

Epps: [Arches her back] Ah, don't remind me.
Cutler: You can always take your shirt off!

Epps: Hey, uh... no.

Cutler: I said shirt, not bra...

Epps: I gotta piss. [She stands up]

Cutler: Carla, c'mon, I was just—

[Eckbaum glares at Cutler and walks around the board off-screen.]

4:30 PM: [Cutler walks toward the camera and away from Eckbaum's front door, which closes behind him, and drops three envelopes on the entryway table.]

Cutler: Mail's here!

Eckbaum: [Behind camera] Oh hey, thanks!

[Cutler flaps his arms several times.]

Cutler: Ah, damn it... you think a shower counts as scratching?

Eckbaum: If it's rubbing against your skin, it's scratching. Besides, since when do you shower?

Cutler: [Shrugs] You got me. [Looks around] Where's Carla?

Eckbaum: Oh, she's in the bathroom. Said she was feeling kinda nauseous. I think it's... [Whispering] you know. Talk about timing.

Cutler: [The camera follows him as he walks past Eckbaum, grabs a drinking glass, and fills it from a pitcher in the refrigerator.] I'm gettin' queasy too, actually. Probably just the cheese. [Drinks] Whoa, talk about thirsty.
Eckbaum: Wait here, I'm gonna go check on her. Carla?

7:45 PM: [The camera faces the TV and couch. Carla and Eckbaum are playing a video game. Cutler walks out of the kitchen looking at his phone and sits in the recliner.]

Eckbaum: Ah, come on! Nice shot.

Epps: [Visibly uncomfortable] Yeah, sure.

Eckbaum: [Turning to her] What's wrong?

Epps: Well, uh, I haven't itched myself in like eight hours, so there's that.

Eckbaum: Just think, though—a hundred bucks!

Epps: [Chuckles] Goodbye, student loan debt!

[Cutler chuckles as well. A few seconds later, he does again.]

Eckbaum: [To Cutler] What is it?

Cutler: My ex, said she's 'itching to see me.'

Eckbaum: Yeah, maybe not tonight. Sorry, but we've kind of got to keep a controlled environment here. [To the camera] Because science!

[Epps doubles over and cries out.]

Cutler: [Half rising from his seat] Whoa, you okay?

Epps: [She shakes her head] Yeah, I'm... I'm good. There was a real sharp one for a sec in my stomach.

Cutler: [Grunts] No kidding. I just got one on my forearm. That
was weird.

Eckbaum: [Reaching out to the camera] Like I said, the nervous system treats itching very similarly to pain, but the key difference is—

Epps: Can we talk about something else? Please?

9:22 PM: [Cutler's back is to the camera. His height just barely fits the frame as he looks out the living room window in silhouette. Moonlight and city lights are the only illumination, obscuring most of the furniture.]

Eckbaum: Hey, why'd you turn the lights out?

Cutler: I think the light is… just… a little itchy. Making it worse.

Eckbaum: [Stepping forward] Hey, man, have you been… you know? [Eckbaum inhales through his teeth.]

Cutler: Nah, man, not… now. But I do want that Chipotle.

Eckbaum: That's the spirit!

[Rapid footsteps come from behind the camera.]

Epps: [Off-camera, audibly disturbed] Okay, something on me just moved.

[The camera spins around.]

Eckbaum: What?

Cutler: [Off-camera] Huh?

Epps: I was looking in the mirror and something in my shoulder and cheek moved.
Cutler: For real?

Eckbaum: 'Moved' or twitched?

Epps: 'Bulged'!

Cutler: You sure she hasn't been on somethin'?

Eckbaum: Guys, guys… it's just a muscle spasm. [Pointing the camera at himself] Those can happen any time, no matter how much you itch, and they're usually nothing to worry about! However, if you are worried, light stretching and lots of water should clear it right up.

Epps: [Off-camera] Will, I've been drinking water all night! I think I wore out your filter.

Cutler: [Off-camera] Uh, me too.

Eckbaum: Look, if it was anything serious, you'd have to have itched yourself by now, right?

10:00 PM: [The camera moves back and forth around the living room. Cutler waves his arms deliriously, twitching and shaking.]

Eckbaum: Okay, uh, ha! It is officially ten o'clock, and Anthony and Carla are... powering through the home stretch!

Epps: Ahh... shut up, shut up, just stop talking, stop everything.

Cutler: Shit, it literally feels like someone's stabbing me now. It's like little knives. Ah! Son of a bitch!

Epps: I'm gonna wait out the rest of it in the bedroom. Keep the camera out of this. [She sniffs; her eyes are watering.]
Cutler: Ditto.

[The two move toward the bedroom door with short, halting steps.]

Eckbaum: Wait, but... no, c'mon!

Epps: [Labored] Got any... good books lately, Will?

Eckbaum: [Sighs] Yeah, top shelf by the sock drawer. Don't lick your thumb when you turn the pages!

[As Cutler disappears through the doorway, he begins removing his shirt.]

10:52 PM: [Eckbaum stands in front of the camera, which faces him at eye level, in the kitchen. He grips a long knife.]

Eckbaum: [Whispering] Late-night snack. [He turns the camera, revealing jars of peanut butter and grape jelly and two slices of bread on a plate. He looks over his shoulder.] Hey, either of you guys want a sandwich?

[Heavy breathing, cursing, and whimpering can be heard in the background.]

Eckbaum: Eh, more for me. [He reaches behind the camera.]

10:59 PM: [Eckbaum holds the camera close to his face.] So, as a bonus video, I'm going to show you how to make a great gluten-free dessert shake. Step one—

[A deep, loud scream erupts from the background. Eckbaum swings the camera toward the bedroom door.]
Eckbaum: Ant? …Hey, Anthony, you okay in there?

[There is another scream. It continues, and is overlapped by a string of sustained, high-pitched shrieks.]

Eckbaum: Anthony? Anthony! Carla!

[Camera at neck level, Eckbaum sprints to the bedroom door and swings it open. He reaches in and turns on the lights.]

Eckbaum: What the—

[Cutler is sprawled on his stomach in boxer shorts in the middle of the hardwood floor, while Epps is in a bra and panties, lying on the bed facing the doorway. The exposed skin on both of their bodies is completely covered in short, narrow slices gushing blood. Fifteen to twenty shapes resembling thin, finger-length black-and-orange centipedes with whip-like tails appear to rest on or emerge from the wounds on each body.]

Eckbaum: Oh God, oh my fucking—

[A hissing noise begins, and the shapes appear to converge on Eckbaum. The view shoots toward the floor between the two bodies, repeatedly flipping and distorting the image, until it comes to rest facing the doorway. There is a metallic thud and, through smeared blood, Eckbaum flees the frame; his sobs are drowned out by the rising hiss. The last image, before the camcorder apparently succumbs to structural failure, is a series of wriggling dark shapes covering the lens.]

***

Q: Just for the record, William, could you state in full what it is that you believe was responsible for the deaths of Carla Epps and Anthony Cutler?

A: [Sighs] I don't know... Christ, I don't know. I told you already.
They're some kind of... a bug. An insect or parasite or something.

Q: Had you experienced any problems with insects in your apartment building in the past?

A: No, you don't understand, it wasn't an... external thing! It's not like, when you get a fly on your windowsill, or a spider in your bathroom! It came from inside of them!

Q: Okay. Do you know if Carla and Anthony had ingested anything or taken any legal or illegal drugs that might—

A: [Shouting] It's inside all of us! Those things are inside all of us! Don't you get it? That's what itching is when there's nothing on you—it's what keeps them down!

Q: If... what you were saying were true, then wouldn't people who were unable to scratch themselves for... I'm quoting Carla here... 'legitimate' medical reasons, be similarly affected? Say, infants, or coma patients, or even people sleeping for long stretches of time?

Q: Shit, I don't know! I'm not a scientist! Maybe it's some kind of, of... uh, physical feedback response, a symbiotic thing that doesn't start until we get older. Maybe they sleep when we do, communicate with pheromones, camouflage... look, this isn't some hearsay or crazy conspiracy theory! I've got video and audio! My best friends are dead! What more do you want from me?

A: [Clears throat] William, this deposition is designed to gather evidence in preparation for your trial in the event that—

A: You know what, screw you! [To off-camera] This isn't about you finding out the truth; it's about moving me through the system, through the motions. You already got the evidence you wanted, and charged me, and set up your whole case, so this is just... faster. It's about getting me to... itch, isn't it? Itch, itch, itch until I scratch. Well, I can do that.

[Eckbaum jumps up and begins aggressively clawing at his skin and clothes, drawing blood.]

Alvarez: Will!

Q: You try it! You sit there and see how long you last!

[Eckbaum lunges at Dermot and an NYPD officer rushes into the frame, grabbing him from behind.]

Q: Oh my God!

A: Do it! The camera's right there! We've got time!

[As Eckbaum and the officer continue to struggle, Dermot backs up against the wall.]

Alvarez: [Stands] My client is suffering serious psychological trauma, if you injure him, in my firm—

[The officer cuffs Eckbaum and ushers him out of frame.]
THE VIDEOGRAPHER: This deposition is hereby suspended. Going off at 3:05 PM.

***

Originally, Eckbaum's hearing was set for April 5, 2014. However, the State moved to prevent Eckbaum's video from being admitted as evidence, claiming it would be unduly prejudicial and confuse the jury. Furthermore, a subsequent mental examination determined Eckbaum suffered from post-traumatic stress disorder, excoriation disorder, and delusional parisitosis, making him unfit to stand trial. As such, Eckbaum agreed to plead guilty to reduced charges of involuntary manslaughter, obstruction of justice, and resisting arrest, and waived his right to a jury trial. After extended negotiations with State authorities, he agreed to a transfer to the Manhattan Psychiatric Center.

The remaining evidence was confiscated through a warrant from an undisclosed federal agency, including autopsy results suggesting that the decedents' wounds were consistent with minor bone fractures or burst inflammation, as opposed to external lacerations. Still, no single source of ruptures in the cardiovascular, muscular, or nervous system could account for the wounds' unique composition, although Alvarez has urged the bodies be exhumed for further autopsy.

A joint wrongful death suit from the decedents' parents is currently pending, as is a tort claim for assault from Ellen Dermot. No trace of the organisms Eckbaum claims to have seen and recorded has ever been found.

The End.

CASE #38387

PRURITUS
BY TREVOR NEIL WHITE

Trevor Neil White has been reading and writing science fiction, fantasy, and scary stories since childhood. A fan of both thoughtful and nail-biting tales that modernize classic supernatural scenarios, he is inspired by Neil Gaiman and Stephen King in equal measure. A 2016 graduate of Cornell Law School, he previously majored in Honors English and Creative Writing at the University of Washington in Seattle. He has self-published two collections of YA fiction and poetry for print and Kindle: "Distortions" (2010) and "Love&Darkness: Vol. I" (2012), and is currently working on his first novel. His writing has appeared in Centralia College's "Beyond Parallax," UW's "AU" and "Bricolage" journals, and the 2012 edition of Phi Theta Kappa Honor Society's "Nota Bene." His other interests include world travel, music, photography, and all things geeky. He currently lives in New York State.

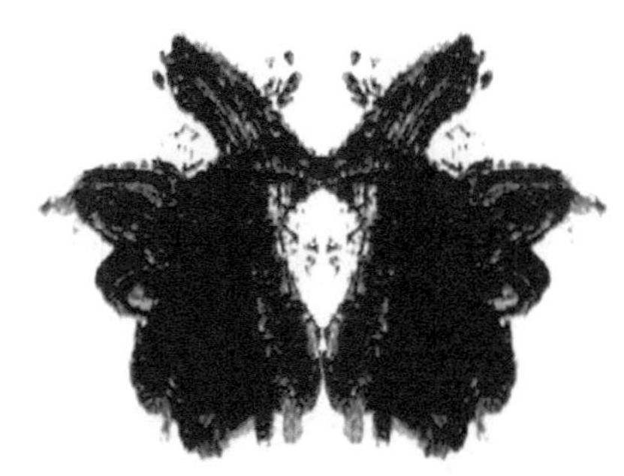

Incursion by Mary Fancher

"Son-of-a-bitch!" Mark jerked his hand off the porch step only to find an inch-long insect hanging onto his palm by its mandibles. He tried shaking the damn thing off, then finally pulled it off, a bit of his skin ripping loose in the process. For a moment, he stared at the creature, now perched aggressively on the porch step. It was the shiny black color of a miniature hearse and somewhat the shape and size of an ant, but not like any ant he had ever seen. The mandibles were a quarter inch long and still working at the bit of flesh it had pulled from his hand.

He picked up one of the running shoes he had been removing and gave the insect a solid whack. "That'll fix you, you little bastard," he said. Feeling vindicated, he picked up the shoe only to find the creature not only still alive, but seemingly unaffected by the force of the blow. It sped off the porch step and into the bushes.

"What happened to you?" Lyla asked as he entered the kitchen. "Damn bug bit me," he said, holding the palm of his left hand out for her to see. Already the bite location was swelling and turning red. You could see the incision where its mandibles had extracted the skin.

"Oh, my God. What got at you? A tarantula? You'd better clean that off and put some antiseptic cream on it." She turned to pour herself a cup of coffee.

"No, not a tarantula." He knew she was joking, but he had expected more sympathy than that. "I was taking my running shoes off and placed my hand on the step. Whammo. It nailed me." She took a sip of coffee and peered once more at the wound. "That looks nasty. I hope there aren't many of what-ever-it-is around."

What a way to start the day, he thought, extracting a mug from an upper cabinet. And one of his least favorite patients was scheduled for the afternoon. Great.

***

He leaned against the back of his chair and tapped the eraser end of his pencil against his lips in an effort to appear interested. Rain was coming down steadily outside the window, creating a hypnotic background against which Mindy Garrett poured out her latest tale of abduction by aliens. He wondered if he should refer her to another therapist since he had been unable to make any headway with her during the past six months. And his patience had begun to run dry.

He surreptitiously glanced at his watch: twelve minutes left in the session. Then another jolt of pain caused him to check his hand again. The entire palm area was red and swollen, and a dull throbbing had begun to work its way up his wrist and into his arm.

"Are you listening to me, Dr. Jacobi?"

With a start, Mark turned his attention back to the young woman, who appeared clearly annoyed. "Yes, I am, Mindy." He could feel his face redden with embarrassment. "I apologize. I was just … just checking my hand." In evidence, he lifted his left arm in the air and turned his palm toward her. "I was bitten by some kind of insect this morning, and I think I'm having a reaction to it."

Now it was Mindy's turn to look embarrassed. "That does look bad," she said. "Maybe you ought to see a doctor." The acne scarred skin over her cheeks took on a purplish red cast, and he was reminded how much he disliked her. "You know, a medical doctor," she added.

He fought his unprofessional feelings toward her—clinical therapists were supposed to be above that, after all—but there was something about her looks and the never-ending tales of woe about alien creatures coming into her bedroom at night that made him ache with revulsion. He had tried his best to suggest the potent symbolism of her "experiences," offer the possibility that what was really going on was merely a symptom of some deeper issue, but she had remained utterly and stubbornly convinced that all of it was real.

He sighed—at both his failure as a therapist and the realization she was right. "I'm afraid I may have to. I've taken a couple of Tylenols, but they haven't even touched the pain." He dropped the pencil onto his desk. "Listen, Mindy. I'm very sorry, but if you don't mind, let's cut this session short. I won't charge you for today. I'm afraid this bite isn't allowing me to concentrate like I should. Do you mind?" Shame formed like a lead weight in the ball of his stomach.

Looking somewhat uncertain, Mindy stood up. "No, I don't mind. As long as I can call you if they return before our next session?" Her eyes held a look of fear that increased his sense of shame.

"Any time," he replied. And he tried to mean it.

***

Dr. Lindstrom held Mark's hand up to the light and bent forward to examine the wound. "You got yourself a bad bite here, Mark. And an allergic reaction, but I think you'll live."

Mark reclaimed his hand. "Thanks, Doc. You didn't tell me anything I didn't already know." He gave the doctor a weak grin.

"I'll write you a script, and I want you to fill it right away. Should help with the pain and swelling." The doctor sat down on a stool and typed away at his laptop. "If you should develop any difficulty breathing, I want you to take yourself to the emergency room immediately. I don't want you to go into anaphylactic shock." He gazed at Mark over his glasses. "Got that?"

Mark nodded. "Do you have any idea what could have done it?"

The doctor closed up the laptop. "What did it look like?"
"Well, it was some kind of insect, you know, six legs. Not a spider. About an inch long and shiny black. Huge pinschers. Almost like little rowels." He looked up at the physician expectantly.

"Sounds like an ant."

Mark shook his head. "I don't think so."

56

Dr. Lindstrom made a face and lifted his hands into the air. "You got me. I'm a medical doctor, not an entomologist. They can all be bad if you have a particular sensitivity to them." He stood up from his stool. "They'll have your script at the desk. Call me if you need to."

***

The three of them were at the dinner table, and Mark was chewing on a mouthful of salad when his wife asked, "Is anything wrong, Mark? You look like you're working your mind overtime." Mark blinked in surprise and swallowed his food. "Just thinking. I'd really like to know what bit me, is all." He glanced down at his hand, still somewhat swollen and painful. "I mean, the little bugger took a piece of my flesh with him. And I slammed my shoe on him and it didn't faze him a bit. You know of an insect that

could do that?" He looked wide-eyed at his wife.

Lyla laughed and poured herself more wine. "Who knows? It's all academic now." Sipping from her wine glass, she continued, "I think you're obsessing over this, Mark. It's a bug bite. Take your medication and you'll feel better tomorrow."

"Who cares, right Dad?" Mark's seven year old son, Casey, grinned up at him, a mouthful of potatoes punching out his cheeks.

"Don't talk with your mouth full." Mark stabbed at a piece of meatloaf.

Casey swallowed and leaned over his plate. "You think you could pitch some balls to me after dinner? Little League camp is next week, and I need to practice."

Mark picked up his wine glass. "I don't know, Casey. Maybe tomorrow. I want to work on the computer tonight. Tomorrow I'll throw you some. Besides, the lawn is still wet from all the rain." He stared down at his plate of food and refused to meet his wife's look.

***

They were watching a movie in the family room—he had paid so little attention to it, he couldn't even remember the name or what it was about—and he had his laptop balanced on his legs. "Do you know there are over 900,000 different species of insects in the world?" he asked out loud.

"Are you going to examine all 900,000 of them until you find the one that bit you?" Lyla's face glowed in the light of the TV screen.

Mark tossed a few kernels of popcorn into his mouth and crunched. "Maybe," he said. "Maybe." He returned his attention to the computer screen.

Nine hundred thousand different kinds of insects, one of which had torn away a chunk of skin and withstood a solid smack from a running shoe. He scrolled down the photos, screen by screen, fascinated by the possibilities but still not recognizing the one he was looking for.

***

The next morning, Mark slept late, luxuriating in the fact that it was Saturday and pretending not to notice when his wife got out of bed at seven. Hoping she would have coffee ready when he eventually came downstairs.

58

He was deep in a dream when a loud scream catapulted him into wakefulness and out of the bed. Rushing into the spare bathroom, he found Lyla and Casey bent over the sink.

"What's the matter? What happened?" he shouted.

Casey was wailing. "It hurts. Get if off me." Lyla looked up at Mark in alarm.

"Let me see." He pushed in between them. Latched onto his son's finger was an insect, identical to the one that had bitten him the day before, its six legs wagging frantically for traction, its fierce mandibles firmly embedded in Casey's flesh. Blood flowed from the wound.

"He's bleeding," Lyla said. "And it won't let go." Mark could tell she was struggling to remain calm.

"Now, stop moving." He held on to Casey's index finger firmly in one hand and pulled at the shiny black insect with the other, but the creature resisted.

No insect can be this tough, he thought, almost starting to panic himself. He tried pinching it between his thumb and forefinger, but all this seemed to do was inspire the creature to latch on more tightly. Casey let out another piercing shriek.

"Wait here," Mark said, racing off downstairs. A minute later he was back with a lighter. "Now, Casey, I want you to remain perfectly still, o.k.? I'm going to light this little guy up so he'll release his grip. Got that?" Mark waited until his son nodded, tears streaming down his face.

"All right. Here goes."

He placed his thumb in between the insect and his son's skin and flicked the switch. "Hold still now," he shouted as Casey jerked his arm back. But the flame had done its job; the insect dropped to the floor. Immediately, Mark placed a water glass upside down on it. He thought he could hear it growling—if insects could do such a thing—from within its glass enclosure.

Lyla was fussing over Casey, washing the wound under running water as the boy continued to cry in pain and fear.

"Don't move that glass," Mark ordered them. "I'm going to get something to put it in. We'll find out just what kind of insect this is." He ran out of the room and down the stairs again.

When he returned, his wife was attaching a Band-Aid over the bite on the boy's finger. "You'll feel better in a few minutes," she cooed. Casey continued to stare in terror at the glass enclosed insect.

Kneeling down, Mark placed a plastic container and a small piece of cardboard down on the floor beside the overturned glass. The insect was throwing itself at the smooth glass walls in what appeared to be a fit of anger. But that was ridiculous, he thought. Insects don't feel anger. "Be careful, Mark," Lyla said from above him. "Whatever you do, don't let it escape."

"I won't." He took the piece of cardboard in his right hand and placed the plastic container on its side next to the glass. With one swift motion, he removed the glass and swept the insect into the plastic container, immediately closing it up with the lid. "There," he shouted triumphantly. "I'll take a picture of that sucker later and we'll find out exactly what it is."

"Can it escape?" Casey asked, his eyes still damp with tears. "Naw," Mark said, holding the plastic container in one hand and giving his son a hug with the other. "It can't get out of here. See?" He gave the container a shake. The insect bounced off the plastic sides and then gripped the bottom, buzzing its defiance.

"I'll put it downstairs on the window sill in the kitchen for now. It's not going anywhere."

***

It was nearly ten o'clock, and a soft breeze was blowing through the open windows, cooling the room off from the heat of the day. Casey had been in bed for an hour.

"How about I get us some ice cream?" Mark asked. He stood up from his recliner.

"I can get it." Lyla pushed the "pause" button on the remote. Mark held his hand up in the air, stopping her. "No, I need to stretch my legs." He headed for the kitchen, all the while humming the theme from the movie they'd been watching. As he turned on the overhead light, he caught sight of the plastic container on the window sill over the sink.

"Oh, shit."

"What's the matter?" Lyla called out.

"I forgot to take a picture of the bug," he said, pulling a carton of ice cream from the freezer. "I'll do it when I'm done here." He dished out scoops of ice cream into two dishes and walked to the sink to rinse out the serving spoon.

"Well, it isn't going anywhere. You can do it tomorrow." Mark turned on the faucet and glanced at the plastic container, realizing, in alarm, that it was empty. He picked it up and saw that a small hole had been eaten—or dug—out of the side. Tiny bits of clear plastic littered the window sill. *What kind of insect can do that?* In a panic, he glanced all around the sink and counter and even on the floor, thinking foolishly that the zombie insect might be somewhere visible, waiting for him to cage it again. Of course, there was no sign of the creature. He dropped the container into the trash, burying it with pieces of dirty paper towels and an empty vegetable bag, hoping that Lyla wouldn't notice it.

61

"Here," he said, handing a bowl of ice cream and a spoon to his wife. "Enjoy."

***

The phone started ringing at 5:45 a.m. Mark glanced at the caller id and groaned. It was his patient, Mindy Garrett. *How the hell did she get my home phone number? And why on earth is she calling this early on a Sunday morning?* Collapsing back on the pillow, he stared at the ceiling while he listened to her message, another hysterical account of aliens visiting her bedroom.

The lump beside him under the sheets cackled in amusement.

He gave her shoulder a gentle shove.

When the message ended, he closed his eyes and was just on the verge of falling back asleep when the phone started ringing again. He pushed himself into a sitting position on the bed and grabbed the receiver.

"Hello," he said, infusing just enough irritation into the tone of his voice to let Mindy know he was not happy.

A panicked voice responded, "Doctor Jacobi, I am so sorry to bother you like this, but I've got to see you. They came again last night." She sounded like she was hyper-ventilating.

"Mmm-hmm."

She was crying now. Hysterical. "I saw them standing at the foot of the bed, but when I tried to get up, run away, I couldn't move. They took me away to their space ship or whatever the thing is. You remember, I told you how they've taken me there before." *Yes, yes, I remember. How could I forget.* "Yes, you have mentioned it once or twice." "I am so afraid for Darcy. They took me away, and she was in the house alone. I'm so afraid they'll take her one of these days. I mean, it's bad enough for me, but—"

He cut her off. "All right now, Mindy. Take a deep breath. Remember what I said about calming yourself when you think these things are happening to you."

"I don't *think* these things are happening to me, Doctor," she interrupted angrily. "I *know* they're happening to me."

"All right, all right. I'm just saying that you need to calm down. You're making matters worse. Try the breathing exercises I taught you."

"Screw the breathing exercises. They inserted something under the skin on my neck. Right behind the ear."

Lyla had given up on sleep now, too, and was putting on her robe and slippers. It was bad enough Mindy had woken him up, but he was seriously annoyed that the call had disturbed Lyla, as well. Which reminded him …

"Mindy, why did you call me on my personal line? I gave you the number to call if there was an emergency."

"I tried that number and left a message, but I needed to speak with you now. I couldn't wait for you to get back to me. You need to see this … this thing on my neck."

He sighed. "What's the thing look like, Mindy?"

Sniffling. "I can't see it real well because, like I said, it's behind my ear. But it feels like a hard lump maybe an inch and a half long." She paused to blow her nose.

"Mindy, I know you're afraid and you're upset, but what makes you think it's not just a bug bite? I get them all the time. In fact, I had a nasty one when I saw you last week. I had to go to my doctor after our appointment, it was so bad. That's probably what woke you up." He thought for a moment. "Do you know there are over 900,000 species of insects in the world?"

"It. Is. Not. An. Insect. Bite." She was clearly overwrought. "When I touch the bump, I can feel something move in there. I'll show it to you. You can see for yourself."

"This sounds more like something your regular physician should look at. Maybe you should go to the emergency room or one of those quick-stop doctor places."

"It's not infected. It's not a bite. I want *you* to see it. This will prove that everything I've been telling you about these aliens is true. Can I please see you for just a few minutes this morning? Twenty minutes? Fifteen?" Her voice had taken on a pleading tone.

He rubbed his forehead with his fingers. "I'm afraid I can't, Mindy. I've got plans I made weeks ago and can't get out of." He hoped the god of therapists would forgive him the lie. "If you can come to my office tomorrow at seven, before my usual office hours, I'll see you then. Meantime, I really think you ought to have a physician check out—."

She hung up.

He set the phone back down on the nightstand and stared at the floor.

"Who was that?" Lyla asked, placing a strong emphasis on the word "that." She placed a cup of black coffee on the nightstand.

"Just my crazy patient who thinks extra-terrestrials come down to visit her from time to time."

She leaned over and deposited a kiss in the middle of his forehead. "Well, this *intra*-terrestrial would like to visit you right now."

He lifted the sheets and gave her a lascivious grin. "Come along, my little earthling."

***

Later in the day, when Lyla and Casey had left the house to do some shopping, Mark removed the hedge trimmer from the garage and went out in the yard to trim a few of the bushes. He enjoyed work like this, pure physical activity that involved little thought and no stress. He often thought he should have gone into landscaping for a profession instead of psychotherapy. Something more peaceful.

He was reaching up to trim a few straggly branches from a lilac tree when he was stunned by a sharp pain in the back of his leg near the ankle. Nearly dropping the trimmer, he turned to check his leg out and felt another biting pain—what felt like the tip of a sharp knife digging into his flesh.

He peered down to see another of the strange insects latched onto his skin. He gave it a firm swat with his hand to brush it off, but the creature hung on defiantly, all the while emitting the faint growling sound.

Unnerved, Mark ran back to the garage where he had stored a can of gasoline. He aimed the spout of the container over the insect and poured a stream of liquid over it. The gasoline ran down his leg and pooled onto the floor of the garage. Gradually, the angry buzzing sound stopped, and the insect loosened its hold on his leg and dropped to the floor. Mark lunged forward to stomp it with his foot, but the bug was too fast. It zipped away into one of the cracks in the foundation.

His leg was throbbing now, and he walked back out into the sunshine to examine the wound.

"Oh, no." Blood was streaming from a small gouge in his leg. It appeared that the zombie bugs weren't just after blood, but were actually eating flesh. "This just can't be," he said out loud. He went into the house to clean and bandage the wound.

Now he was angry. No, furious might be a better word. When he was done patching up the wound, he returned to the garage with a can of Raid. "Take this you little bastards." With an almost diabolical pleasure, he sprayed the crack where the insect had disappeared and all along the bottom walls of the garage. Then he took the can and returned to where he had left the hedge trimmer in the yard and began to survey the ground for signs of more of the little horrors.

As he wandered about the yard, his attention was drawn to a dark lump by the back fence, something he hadn't noticed before.

Walking up to it, he realized it was a dead squirrel. Intestines protruded from its pale belly, and two of its ribs were partially visible where something had begun to eat it.

Thinking it must have been killed by the neighbor's cat, he gave the dead animal a soft shove with his foot to turn it over. When a handful of the zombie bugs ran out from inside the carcass, he stepped back in horror.

"Holy fuck." He was so stunned by the implications that he didn't even try to capture one before they fled.

"That's no language for a Sunday, Mark."

Mark looked up to see his neighbor standing on the other side of the fence, grinning at him.

"What's wrong?"

"I'm not sure, Glenn," Mark answered, shaking his head. "Have you seen any odd-looking bugs around, about an inch long with wicked looking mandibles? They bite like a son-of-a-bitch. Look at this." He turned around and lifted the bandage. "And this." He raised his hand to display the first bite, just beginning to heal.

"Wow, a bug did that? Are you sure you weren't attacked by a miniature schnauzer?" Glenn tossed his head back and laughed. Mark covered the bite back up.

"No, I can't say I've seen anything unusual," Glenn continued. "Just spiders and mosquitoes and such. Oh, and carpenter ants. Are you sure it wasn't a carpenter ant? They're big and they can give a nasty bit if so inclined."

Mark was still thinking about the squirrel. "No, it wasn't a carpenter ant. Guess I'll have to call the exterminators tomorrow morning. Whatever they are, I've got to get rid of 'em." He started to walk away.

"Say, Mark," Glenn called out. "Speaking of nasty critters, you haven't seen our cat Lucky in the past day or two, have you? You know, he's the black one with one white paw? He always comes home every evening for his dinner, like clockwork. We haven't seen him now for two, three days. He's never done this, and Becky is worried."

Mark felt the color drain from his face. He almost told Glenn about the squirrel and what he thought might have killed it, but decided not to. No one would believe an insect could kill a squirrel, much less a cat. He wasn't even sure he did.

"No," he said. "I haven't seen him, but I'll bring him right over if I do."

"Thanks, Mark. Becky and I would appreciate it. Oh, and Mark?"

"Yeah, Glenn?"

"About the bugs, you know what it says in the Bible. The meek shall inherit the earth." Glenn gave him a big grin.

"These things aren't meek."

He scooped up the dead squirrel with a spade and slid the remains into a black trash bag which he sprayed with Raid and dropped in the trash can. By now, the whole garage was filled with a nauseous mix of gasoline and bug spray, but this was a small price to pay in order to keep the nasty insects away. He was staring out at the yard and contemplating what more he could do, when he heard his wife's car pull into the driveway. As he turned around to greet them, his son Casey exploded out of the car and ran into the garage.

"Look what Mom got me at the store," he called out, pointing toward the Subaru where his mother was struggling to remove something out of the back.

"What?" Mark grinned.

"It's a Surf 'n Slide," Lyla said as he went to help her with a large box. "It was on sale, and I couldn't resist. You inflate it and fill the bottom with water and—oh, I don't know. It looked like a fun way for Casey to cool off in the backyard." By this time they had brought the box into the garage and set it on the floor.

"Oh, my God," Lyla said, straightening up. "This place stinks. What have you been doing?" She covered her nose with her hand.

"Nothing. I just found a couple more of those bugs and sprayed the shit out of them."

"Sshhhh." Lyla inclined her head toward Casey, who was studying the photograph of the Surf 'n Slide on the box. "Casey, you go out in the backyard now. Daddy and I will set up the slide in a couple of minutes. I don't want you to breathe these fumes in." Mark suddenly panicked. "Casey, no. Why don't you go inside and watch some TV? We'll set the Surf 'n Slide up later. Maybe tomorrow."

The boy halted in mid-step, his face a tortured mask of childhood disappointment. "I don't want to go inside. Mom said we could put it up now."

"What do you mean, maybe tomorrow?" Lyla looked at him accusingly. "It's ninety degrees out and a beautiful, sunny day. Why does he have to wait until tomorrow?" The boy began to wail. She raised her eyes heavenward and turned away.

Mark grabbed her by the arm. The last thing he wanted to do was scare her, but until he knew more about what was going on with the insects, he couldn't risk Casey being attacked again. "Lyla," he said in a whisper that could barely be heard over the child's wailing. He licked his lips nervously. "I just don't want him to play in the yard today. Maybe for the next few days."

"Why?"

"Just trust me for now."

For a moment she stared at him as if the answer to the mystery might suddenly pop out of his ears or emerge from his mouth like a cartoon balloon.

"All right," she finally said. "All right. But there better end up being a good reason, because Casey's working himself up into a state right now."

"I hope there isn't a good reason," Mark mumbled as she walked away to comfort Casey. "I really hope there isn't."

***

He woke earlier than usual Monday morning without knowing quite why. He swung his legs over the side of the bed and sat staring into the shadows. The room was mostly dark, gray fingers of pre-dawn light just beginning to slide around the edges of the curtains. He could hear the sound of rain falling steadily against the roof. *Another rainy day.*

It felt like something was wrong. Something within the shadows or behind the furniture. Something within the rain. And then he realized what it was. A faint buzzing sound almost like a bee or fly caught in a jar, but louder and not quite the same. He cocked his head, but even as he tried to pin it down, the sound disappeared. Finally, he gave up and went downstairs.

He stared sleepily out the kitchen window while he waited for the coffee maker to finish, thinking how he wouldn't be going for a run that day what with the rain and all. Wondering again what it was he heard that woke him up.

The coffee maker was just finishing its cycle when he thought he heard the sound again, but this time he could tell it was coming from the garage. Fearing there might be a bird or small animal that had gotten caught there by mistake, he opened the door just a crack, but was nearly bowled over by the overpowering stench of something dead. He turned on the garage light and cautiously walked around the cement floor. The stench and the noises seemed to be concentrated in one of the corners.

"Ahh, no." The neighbor's cat lay motionless on the cement flooring behind the lawnmower, tufts of black fur sticking to a pool of blood beneath it. The body seemed to be moving, writhing, as if the cat were still alive, but when he realized what was causing the movement, he backed away in revulsion. Grabbing a nearby rake, he pushed the tines against the dead cat. Immediately, a phalanx of the zombie insects left their feast and headed in his direction.

Barefoot and in briefs, he had no choice but to retreat inside the house. He rushed to slip on a pair of sandals, grabbed a can of bug spray and a jar, and returned to the garage. He paused at the top of the steps and surveyed the cement floor, ready to leap into action.

But the zombie insects had disappeared.

He stepped slowly down the steps, glancing from side to side as he walked toward the dead cat. Still no bugs. Even the carcass seemed to have been abandoned. He gave it a shove with the rake, just to be sure, but there was no sign of any of them.

Frustrated, he strode around the perimeter of the garage, pushing boxes and tools about in an effort to flush them out, but the creatures seemed to have disappeared into thin air. Finally, he shoveled the cat carcass into a plastic bag and placed it in the trash can, then wheeled the can out to the street, thanking God it was trash day. He wondered if he should tell his neighbors about what happened to their cat, but decided against it. Better they didn't know.

His wife was in the kitchen when he returned inside, her eyes opening wide at the sight of him in his boxer shorts and sandals and soaking wet from the rain. "You went outside that way?"

He ran a hand through his rain drenched hair. "Yeah, why?" In reply, she wrinkled her nose up. "Have you been spraying with Raid again? What are you trying to do, poison us?" She stared at him as if he had lost his mind, which, in fact, he was close to believing himself.

"Oh, I thought I saw another one of those insects that bit me and Casey," he said in as calm a voice as he could muster. He fought against the urge to share his fears with her, but before he did that, he needed to find out how he could get rid of them. "As long as I was out there taking the trash out, I thought I'd do a little spraying. Today's garbage day, you know." He poured himself a cup of coffee and headed for the stairs.

"Is anything wrong, Mark?"

He paused in the doorway. "No. Nothing at all." And he went upstairs to take a shower.

***

He arrived at his office well before seven, wondering if Mindy Garrett would show up, almost hoping she wouldn't. While he waited, he made himself a cup of coffee and searched the Internet for local exterminators.

Mindy arrived on time, but Mark could tell from the way she shook the moisture from her umbrella and barely glanced his way that she was annoyed. Probably because he had refused to see her on Sunday. Too bad, he thought.

Mark waited for her to start, but when she sat staring at her fingernails without saying a word, he was forced to begin. "You seem calmer today."

Her eyes briefly connected with his and then drifted downwards again. She shrugged.

For the first time, Mark realized that there was a large square bandage behind one of her ears. "I see your ear is bandaged," he said. "Is that what you called me about Sunday morning?"

He thought he saw a flash of anger in her face when she said, "Yes, it is."

He stood up and stepped around the desk. "Do you mind if I take a look?"

Mindy put her fingers up to the bandage and winced. "It's gone now. The lump, I mean, and what was in it. Now there's just the wound."

"What happened?"

"I told you Sunday morning," she answered sullenly. "They came for me again and when I woke up, I found a lump on my neck. When I touched it, I could feel something move inside. Every time I touched it, the thing moved." She shivered at the memory. "Around noon, I started feeling intense pains there, and blood began to seep from it. When I looked in the mirror, something was crawling out of the lump."

"Something?"

"Yes. An insect. Only I don't think it was an insect. It looked more like a robotic version of an insect; you know?"

He said nothing.

Carefully, Mindy pulled back the bandage, displaying a raw, gaping hole in her flesh. "That's what it did to me to get out."

Mark's eyes widened in horror. "Did you go to the emergency room like I said?"

She glared at him. "And if a doctor asks me how I got it, what should I say? That I was abducted by space aliens and they implanted this creature in my neck and it ate its way out? Do you think a doctor is going to believe me any more than you have?"

Mark immediately felt a rush of guilt and returned to his seat behind the desk. He was stricken with the terrible idea that this might somehow be connected with his zombie bugs, but that was patently ridiculous. Shaking the thought from his mind, he asked, "So what happened to the insect? Did you kill it?"

She shook her head and, digging into her purse, pulled out a glass jar with a heavy lid and placed it on his desk.

He leaned forward and realized to his horror that the jar contained one of the same insects he had been doing battle with the whole weekend. "What's it doing?" The insect was resting along one side of the bottom of the jar, its thorax throbbing. Tiny, iridescent globules were spread out behind it.

"It's laying eggs," she said, as if the answer should be obvious. "It's laying eggs so it can create more like itself. When I first put it in the jar, it threw itself against the sides and hissed up a storm. After a while, it grew quiet and lay still, and now you see what it's doing."

She stood up and swung the strap of her purse over her shoulder. "Now do you believe what I've been trying to tell you for months? I'm not schizophrenic. I'm not delusional. This is your proof. The aliens abducted me because they want me to be a vehicle for them. And I'm sure I'm not the only person they've used in this way."

Mindy walked toward the door, but paused with one hand on the door knob. "I won't be coming back any more, Dr. Jacobi. I finally realized you can't help me. Perhaps no one can. But you need to know that this creature was put it in me for a reason. I don't know what the reason is right now, but I'm afraid I will before long. I'm afraid we'll all know. And I doubt it's going to be a good thing."

Mark watched her walk out the door, a cold, sinking feeling filling his gut. He forced himself to pick up the glass jar. As he held it up to the light, the zombie insect popped out another of the iridescent eggs. Then it turned to look at him.

The End

CASE #13867

INCURSION

BY MARY FANCHER

Mary Fancher is an artist and writer living in Baldwinsville, New York with her husband and four irritating cats. She possesses a degree in studio art from the State University of New York at Binghamton, and has displayed her art work in a number of galleries and juried exhibitions in New York, Oregon, and South Carolina.

Her writing has included work in both historical fiction and horror. JOHN LEE, a work of historical fiction, was one of the finalists for the 2014 South Carolina First Novel Award. Another historical fiction novel, THE LOVE LETTER OF JOHN HENRY HOLLIDAY, was on the short list for the 2015 Historical Novel Society's Indie Editor's Choice Award, and can be purchased on Amazon. A short story, THE POTATO FIELD, was recently published in an anthology by The Horror Zine.

Mary is currently working on a third novel that is a cross-over piece of historical fiction with elements of magic mixed in.

CASE #: 55019

Inmate by Michael Fassbender

Today a new team of doctors comes to this madhouse. From a window on the third floor, I watch them carry their strange equipment out of the vehicle that brought them to our door. I see the master of the facility opening the door to usher them inside. They gaze up at the impressive facade of this institution, taking it all in as they walk. If any takes notice of me, there is no sign. It is always the same, I tell myself. They think they understand us better than we understand ourselves. They tell us they can help us. Some even claim that they can help us to solve our problems and leave this place for good. What they really want is to study us. With our help, they can make some grand discovery that will etch their names into the annals of science forever. The staff here know better. They have seen so much, and they know that we are as we are. They harbor no illusions of curing us any longer. They fulfill their obligations, and no more. It seems that I can go for days now without seeing a nurse or orderly.

The doctors who visit are different. Their faces glow with expectation. They bring their ever-stranger instruments, their confidence, their eager and hungry eyes, always yearning for that breakthrough that will assure their fame. Resigned to the inevitable, the staff here permits it. As for my fellow patients, it differs for each of us. Some withdraw, while others play along. I do not cooperate for long. I am known for this. Still the doctors hope to win my assent, all the more because it is rarely given.

The three young doctors who have come today begin on the ground floor, of course. There is much ground to cover. Sometimes their fellows even pay a visit to the basement before climbing the stairs to the upper levels. I know that there will be some time before they come to me, so I shuffle back to my room to wait. It is always so predictable, so banal, that I wonder how I will muster the energy to endure their attentions.

In due time I hear them in the adjacent room. They are always so polite. Do they teach that in medical school? They ask my neighbor for her permission to speak with her. What would they do, should she refuse? I wonder. They would likely maintain the pretense that she had granted their request. These are thorough; they ask her to allow them to take pictures. I think back for a moment to their arrival. I do not recall seeing them carrying camera equipment inside. Of course, their instruments change much with passing years. I remind myself that cameras are no longer as large as they had been. One person could carry several, and here are three.

I wonder if my neighbor is even listening to them as they prate on. With or without a response, they recite their litany of questions. Two take the lead, the woman and one man, while the other man attends to their instruments and only occasionally remarks on his findings. He is so specialized that his comments are unintelligible to any who is not a part of their team. Kaytoo is reading green? Either they think that we are but children, or perhaps they belong here as patients, not doctors.

At last I hear them bidding my neighbor farewell, and they quit her room for mine. I am not impressed. Doctors have become slovenly of late, dressing more like workmen than responsible professionals. They are a woman and two men. The woman leads them with some unspoken authority, though her flannel shirt and denim trousers suggest a career in farming. The first man wears a green coat of some light material and stained trousers that seem to be light brown when clean. The second man seems to favor black, perhaps because he prefers to linger in the shadows of the other two. He must be important, however, for each hand carries a small instrument. In his right hand is a small box with a lens, more likely some kind of camera than a telescope or microscope, while his left holds a longer box. Two green lights glow on its upper surface; as he enters the room, a yellow one turns on.

"Kaytoo reads yellow," is the man's response. The other man and the woman exchange glances. I wait as their eyes dart about the room. No one deigns to look at me directly.

The woman speaks first. "May we talk to you?" I consider saying no, at least until they acknowledge me more directly. There are some moments of silence, apart from the occasional pulse sounded by Kaytoo. These slow a bit as the yellow light in the middle disappears. The man holding it starts to say something, but stops as the other man speaks.

"We mean no harm," he begins in a surprisingly cultured, British voice. "We simply wish to pose you a few questions."

The woman speaks again, her own voice marking her as a native to our area. "The first is can we take pictures?"

You *may*, I think. I say nothing, but wave my hand to show my indifference. I note with interest that a yellow light on Kaytoo flickers. The British man turns his head, glances at the instrument, and then nods to the other man. The latter raises the small box in his right and touches something on its side. Looking intently at something in the box, he moves it around slowly, pointing its lens in every direction in turn. I glare at him for a moment.

The British man pulls a small box from his pocket, and says, "I have a recorder here." It seems small for a proper dictaphone. "If you've anything to say, say it to the recorder." He holds this box away from his body, heedless once again of my actual position.

Her eyes darting in all directions, the woman asks, "Would you like to tell us your name?" I laugh. The yellow light on Kaytoo flickers again. What is it doing? The woman whispers to her companions something about Evie P., surely a mutual acquaintance. I know nothing of her, however, and I am not amused. Professionals should not carry on in this way. The yellow light appears again, and this time it remains lit.

The woman speaks again. "Why are you here?" I am annoyed by the excitement in her voice. She must know my file. It can only be some sick doctor's trick, and she is enjoying it far too thoroughly.

That is not right. Only tragedy brings a person here. My baby. No.

No! Tones accelerate. "Orange!"

They manipulate me. They prod at my very soul, and for what? Some marks on a chart? I will remain silent, whatever they say. My cooperation has ended.

The tones slow again. "Yellow." A pause. "No, green."

Far too loudly, the woman cries out to the air, "Wait! Come back!"

The British man lowers his tiny dictaphone and says, "Please. We can help you."

I have heard that lie often enough. I maintain my composure, and regard them coldly, hoping that they will leave.

The British man turns to the woman and says, "Sorry, Jess, but I'm a cheeky bastard." He turns to regard the room again, and says, "You do know that you've died, right?"

What manner of game?

Cheeky Bastard is not finished. "How did you die? When?"

I scream at them, "Get out of here! Now!" The tones accelerate to a new crescendo. "Leave me in peace!"

The man in black cries out, "Red!" He lowers his camera to capture Kaytoo with all five bulbs lit.

Jess looks at Cheeky Bastard with what seems like raw admiration. Without taking her eyes from him, she asks, "Is it all right if we ask more questions?"

Cheeky Bastard asks her, "Do you feel it?"

Jess pulls a small box from her pocket, prods at it a few times, and says, "It's dropped at least seven degrees."

"I think this spirit has tendered its consent." Cheeky Bastard seems very pleased with himself. "Again, if you've anything to say, please say it to my recorder. We can listen later.""Are you a man or a woman?" Jess speaks quickly, even before Cheeky Bastard finishes. Competition? "What is your name?" She pauses. "What year do you think it is?"

"Did you come here willingly, or were you committed?" Cheeky Bastard grins as he waits. I cringe. The lights flicker a bit on Kaytoo, and he smiles even more broadly. "Tell me what was wrong." Several seconds, as if he expects a detailed response. "How did you die?"

No more!

I muster my strength for a backhanded blow to his precious recorder. Jess shrieks as the recorder flies in front of her face. Kaytoo seems to scream with her. Cheeky Bastard rubs his hand and says, "My mobile."

Jess shouts back to the man in black. "Did you get that?" His response is unnecessarily profane. Jess begins to look worried. "I don't think it wants us here anymore."

No Jess, "it" most assuredly does not.

Cheeky Bastard picks up his "mobile" recorder and stares at it sourly. "Let's shove off before it breaks any more of our equipment."

Yes, do.

The man in black lowers his camera. "I don't think we're going to beat what we've already got."

Jess looks around the room slowly. "Yeah, you're probably right." After a moment, she speaks up again more loudly. "Well, thanks for talking to us."

They leave my room, but not the building. I try to ignore them, but when they get to the Day Room on our floor, they make so much noise that I cannot. That room is partially mine. It seems wrong to permit them to abuse it so. I leave my room to follow them discreetly.

At first, they pay me no heed, but Kaytoo is not so oblivious. I wonder how I should feel about this curious device. Should I thank it for acknowledging me or break it for announcing my every move?

For now, I leave it aside. The visitors know that I am here, and begin asking their questions again. I grow angry, and Kaytoo warns them. I must be more careful. I back out of the room, but watch them from outside the doorway. Kaytoo slows down, and the people show disappointment.

I wait. They talk to an empty room. They grow tired of the game. They ignore me as they file back into the hall.

No, Jess shudders as she walks by me.

They nearly tricked me. They would have me believe that I am invisible. Such a sophisticated game. What did they think they could learn? These doctors. It isn't right, the way they take advantage of people. Do they want to make us more disturbed than we are?

They are halfway down the hall from me, but Kaytoo knows how I feel. Perhaps that small instrument is the one I like best of the whole group, after all. Somehow it understands. Plainly the doctors are no good in this respect.

Jess stops and turns around. Kaytoo must have startled her out of her game, because now she looks directly at me. I fix her gaze with mine, and her eyes grow very wide. She must be mortified at her mistake. Good. I smile, very widely. She seems unhappier with every second. I begin to walk toward her.

As I take my fourth step towards Jess, she whispers, "Guys? She's here. She's coming this way."

The men stop. The one dressed in black pushes Kaytoo into one of his pockets and fumbles with his camera. I pick up my pace.

Jess. "Can you see her?" Cheeky Bastard. "Not as such. What do you see?" Jess. "She is coming, and I don't think we want to be there when she gets here." She turns and runs for the staircase.

Smart girl. We're all mad here, of course. Heaven knows what we might do to them if they caught us in a mood.

Cheeky Bastard pauses a moment while the other man bolts after her. He is likely keen to protect that camera and whatever film they can make fit inside it.

That is fine. He is the one I want.

He reaches the staircase as I prepare to strike. Another backhand blow, delivered to his left shoulder blade, sends him tumbling down the stairs. He nearly knocks the other man over in the process, but the latter's sense of self-preservation helps him to maintain his balance. Perhaps it has more to do with protecting his precious instruments.

Cheeky Bastard reaches the bottom even before Jess. He lands hard on his left knee, and screams. The others scurry to help him. "Are you all right?" "What hurts?" I do not care who said what.

Cheeky Bastard tells me all that I wanted to know. "She broke my sodding leg!" I laugh. I would never have guessed that he was a farmhand.

His companions hoist him up between them and help him out the front door. I keep my distance, and anyway, I am more relaxed now. Kaytoo barely registers my presence. Maybe the doctors are too tired to notice.

Jess opens the door of her motor carriage and gestures wildly at the man in black. "Are you sure you want to leave the stuff in the basement?"

Jess waves him on more urgently. "Leave it! We have to get Reggie to a hospital now!" The irony. Besides, I would not touch the rest of their equipment. I have broken enough. Wait. There is nothing to stop me from hopping into the back of their vehicle. I sneak in. If they notice, they pretend not to do so. Somehow, I've escaped!

I stand in the bathroom of a small apartment. Jess is in the bedroom, having an intense conversation with her small device about Reggie and his broken leg. Again, I consider looking at my reflection in the mirror, but I just don't think I will like what I see.

Silence. Her conversation must be over. I step out into the bedroom. More time must have passed than I thought. The room is dark, and she sleeps in her bed. I know that I am a guest, but that is rude. I had intended to thank her for allowing me to stay with her while I got back on my feet.

It is rude to awaken her, but I think she deserves that for ignoring me. It is far more rude to accept her generosity without expressing my gratitude.

So, I stand at her bedside, and reach out to wake her. I will show my appreciation by greeting her with my widest smile.

The End.

CASE #55019

INMATE
BY MICHAEL FASSBENDER

Michael Fassbender is a part-time writer in the Chicago area, and holds Master's Degrees in Modern European History and Russian Studies from Indiana University Bloomington. Apart from his graduate studies and three trips to Europe, he has spent his entire life to date in the suburbs of Chicago.His first literary love is supernatural horror. Poe and Lovecraft inspired him to begin writing in high school, but 2016 marks his first appearance in print media apart from a few college journals. In recent years, he has written a couple of hundred articles for the now-defunct website Helium, mostly in non-fiction. Most of these articles are now available on his website, michaeltfassbender.com, and there is also a short story in the tradition of Poe on the fiction page.

CASE #: 93231

Black Dog by Icy Sedgwick

My name is Samuel Phipps and I offer my position as a clerk within a firm of engineers as testament to my sanity. I can offer no other evidence as to the veracity of the events which I am about to relate, other than the testimony I shall lay before you.

I was staying with my brother in a small Norfolk village; he has been recently married and I had promised to visit with him and his dear wife. On the night before I was due to take my leave, bound once more for London, I visited another friend on the edge of the town. My brother could not make the visit due to illness, and I found myself in a position of having to leave my friend's lodgings without arrangements for transportation being made.

It is not so large a village that one feels compelled to travel by coach, or even horseback, and at that moment in my visit, both were extravagances which I could ill afford. I deemed it prudent to make the short journey on foot, and took my leave of my gracious host. Moments before I left, he offered the suggestion that I might shorten my return journey by some ten minutes or so by cutting through the graveyard, instead of following the meandering lane. I thanked him for his suggestion, and stepped out into the cold March air.

I had not gone three paces when a small hand tugged on my arm. I am not accustomed to frights, or extended indulgence of my imagination, but the suddenness of the act startled me. I looked down and saw that the hand belonged to that of my friend's maid. She had been returning to the house from the chicken coop when she heard my friend's suggestion, and she begged me to ignore the advice, and take my intended route. I told her that I wished to return home and if my friend's suggestion would allow me to do so all the quicker, then I would follow it. She told me that the graveyard was the haunt of the infamous 'Black Shuck', and she pleaded with me to take the longer route, "all the better to avoid 'im". The little maid seemed convinced that my soul would be lost should I encounter the beast, seen only in the graveyard on nights such as these, and I saw no way to placate her that would not involve a lie. I assured her that I would take the long walk instead, and left her clasping her hands in gratitude.

I am not a man prone to such notions, but I regretted my choice the instant I set foot in the graveyard. A narrow gate admitted me in the rear wall, and a winding path cut a swathe between a host of stones. I normally find such places to be fascinating records of human experience, but with a cold wind at my back, and frost in the air, I found I had little time to read the stones. I fancied I heard footsteps, yet when I turned my head, I saw nothing in the moving shadows.

Something howled in the darkness behind me, and I glanced over my shoulder to discover its source. The path was empty. I heaved a sigh of relief and turned back to the path ahead. A large black dog blocked my way. Around three feet high, it stood perhaps seven yards away, with ragged fur and enormous paws. Red eyes burned in its impassive face; its features akin to those of a mastiff. It did not snarl, or bare its teeth as I feared it would. It regarded me with vague interest, but I sensed no real malice on its part. I recalled the fevered words of the maid and wondered if this was the Black Shuck of which she spoke. I found I could not move, bound to the spot as I was with fright.

The dog walked along the path towards me, carrying itself with the dignity one more associates with cats than dogs. It regarded me all the while with its red eyes, and I could not even close my own to prevent my seeing its approach. Some nefarious agency kept my eyes wide open. The dog sniffed my hand in the manner of any normal hound, and lifted its gaze to meet my own. I saw nothing in its eyes, no danger or evil, nor willful defiance of the Lord. The dog simply…was.

With no warning, it stood on its hind legs, and pressed its paws against my chest. I would have started for I felt no weight behind the gesture, no sudden movement that may cause me to stumble backward. The dog gazed into my eyes, and let out a single bark. An instant later, my eyes closed and I regained control of my limbs. When I opened my eyes, the dog was gone, and I was alone in the graveyard.

I hurried home, and arrived at the same moment that I surely would have done had I taken the longer route. I did not tell my brother or his wife of my ordeal, and I retired to bed, pleading a headache. I did not wake for two days, and when I finally did awake, my brother's wife explained in halting terms that the coach I was to have taken overturned on the journey, killing its occupants.

I returned to London a day later, somewhat fearful of the coach, and discovered that a fire destroyed my lodgings on the day I should have returned. A host of such tales played out before me, and soon my acquaintances congratulated me on my run of good fortune. I smiled and shook their hands, agreeing in turn, but I could not bring myself to speak of the events in the graveyard, nor tell of the two mysterious marks that had appeared on my chest, marks shaped like those of cloven hooves.

The End.

CASE #:93231

BLACK DOG

BY ICY SEDGWICK

By day, Icy teaches design students how to use the Adobe software, and advertising students how to write copy. She's also working on a PhD, looking at set design in haunted house films. By night she becomes Icy and she writes a lot of weird fiction. She's had several stories included in a range of genre anthologies, including Suspended in Dusk, European Monsters, Short Stack, Masks and Bloody Parchment: Beachfront Starter Home, Good Bones. She also knits up a storm and makes jewellery!

Her first book, a pulp Western named The Guns of Retribution, was published in May 2013, and its weird Western sequel, To Kill A Dead Man, came out in January 2016. Her horror fantasy novella, The Necromancer's Apprentice, was published in 2014. She's currently writing its sequel, The Necromancer's Rogue, with plans for a third in the series! You can find her on Twitter @IcySedgwick, or read her free fiction at www.icysedgwick.com.

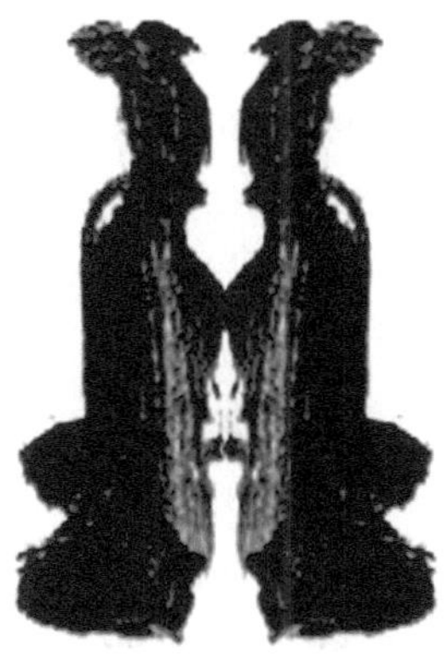

The Can by Kyle Bakke

Warren Carter was walking down a lonely stretch of Iowa road when he got caught in the middle of a winter storm. As the snow piled high on the ground and the icy wind howled its fury, he scanned the path ahead and behind him in the hopes that a car might come by. The last ride he'd hitched had gotten him out of Illinois before dropping him off in a small town – Mavern if he remembered right – ten miles back. Since then, he'd continued west on foot. Someday he hoped to make it Vegas, where it never got too cold, for a Midwesterner anyway, and there were always tourists to mooch off of. But he'd be lucky to reach the next county if he wasn't able to flag down a ride soon. Already he could envision some farmer stumbling across his frosty blue corpse after the spring thaw.

He kept walking. No matter how desolate the area he was in was, sooner or later a car had to drive by. Of course, there was the chance that if a vehicle passed him its driver wouldn't stop and offer him a ride. He tried to tell himself that that was ridiculous, that they'd have to at least drive him someplace to find shelter, or he'd freeze to death. Then again, how many people had told him to piss off when he'd asked them if they could spare a few bucks so he could order something off the dollar menu at McDonald's instead of digging through the garbage for rancid food scraps? But even if he wasn't able to land a ride, there had to be a farmhouse along this road somewhere. And surely any farmer in rural Iowa would be a God Fearing-Salt-Of-The-Earth type who'd consider it their Christian duty to play the role of Good Samaritan if he came to their door.

Another mile passed, and there still wasn't a car in sight. To make matters worse, the temperature was dropping as night fell, and while Warren was bundled up for the weather, his clothes were old and worn. His sneakers were the worst; they had holes in them, and the cold that seeped in were beginning to make his toes feel numb. His fingers weren't faring any better, because his gloves were made of a thin material. Even beneath his orange stocking cap his ears were starting to feel chill.

Up until this point, the one consolation Warren could take in his current situation was that the wind was at his back, but then the wind shifted and he found himself walking into the teeth of a fierce gale. The wind seemed to drive icy needles into his cheeks, and he had to lower his face in order to press on.

Up ahead the road rose in a camel-like hump, and when Warren crested the rise and glanced down its slope, he saw the dark silhouette of an old house at the bottom of the hill. No lights shone in the home's windows. No vehicles were park nearby. Once he got closer, Warren could see why.

The house was abandoned.

Which was just as well, Warren figured. With no owner, he couldn't be turned away at the door, nor would anyone care if he let himself in, if only for a night to wait out the storm.

His spirits lifted, Warren quickened his pace and marched the short distance that separated him from his sanctuary.

As it is with so many things, time had been cruel to the house. Most of its windows were broken. Its front porch sagged, and following years of neglect, a large portion of its roof had caved in. But as dilapidated as the home was, Warren thought it would last another night if it'd stood for this long.

Once inside, Warren was immediately relieved of the unforgiving wind, but he had trouble seeing anything in the darkness that ruled the house. Placing a hand against the wall, he made his way into one of the rooms that flanked the entryway. Here some of the darkness gave way to faint moonlight that filtered through the storm clouds outside to spill through the room's shattered windows. In the dim glow, Warren could make out a tattered couch with stuffing spilling from its cushions and an overturned TV with a busted screen.

Were it not for the broken windows, which let in the screaming wind, Warren would have plopped down on the couch and gone to sleep, but he would just as likely freeze in this room as he would have had he stayed outside. He needed to find a room without windows if he was ever going to find some real warmth.

Leaving the den, Warren found himself in another room. A kitchen, he realized, after spotting a rusty stove and a toppled refrigerator. Here, too, the wind came swirling through windows behind the sink, carrying with it snow and bitter cold.

Before venturing on to the next room, Warren went through the cupboards in case there might be any food in them. As he suspected, the shelves were bare. But it was in his search for something to eat, that he came across a door that let into a pantry.

When he opened the pantry door, a shrieking rat burst from the small closet-sized room before darting off into the darkness, damn near startling Warren to death. Even as he laughed off the incident, Warren realized how terrified most people would be were they in his place. Here he was, in the middle of nowhere, at night in an abandoned house all by himself. It was the stuff horror movies were made of. But Warren knew all too well that horror movies were made for people who had little to truly fear in their lives. These people weren't homeless drifters. They didn't have to worry about where their next meal would come from, or where they would lay their heads down at night. They had jobs and homes, and loved ones to care for them, which is why it was acceptable for them to fear things that go bump in the night. Warren didn't have that luxury; the only boogeyman he faced at that moment was the storm that raged outside.

But on the bright side, it looked like the pantry would serve his purpose. It was completely enclosed, and would offer him total protection from the wind.

Stepping inside the pantry, Warren closed the door behind him and sat on the floor. Then, leaning his back against the wall, he folded his arms across his chest and tucked his hands beneath his armpits. It took a while, but gradually some of the chill went out of him.

As soon as he felt warm enough, Warren removed his gloves and began rummaging through his knapsack. When his fingers brushed the matchbook he'd gotten from a strip joint in Moline, he pulled it from the bag and struck one of the matches. With no wind to disturb it, the match burned strong, and before Warren burnt his fingers and had to shake the match out, he saw that, unlike the cupboards in the kitchen, the pantry's shelves weren't empty.

Lighting another match, Warren examined the pantry shelves and saw three items: a half-melted candle, a kitchen knife, and a tin can.

Warren grabbed the candle, lit it, and placed it on one of the shelves; it made the pantry almost feel cozy. Next, he took the can. It was covered in rust and bore no label. But it did feature a pull tab, so he wouldn't have any trouble opening it.

Warren was just getting ready to do so when the can trembled in his hands.

The vibration only lasted a second before the can went still. The strange occurrence happened so quickly that Warren doubted it even took place. More likely, he reasoned, his hands had been shaking because they were still cold. Much like the incident with the rat, Warren shrugged off any thought of the can moving in his hands. Now he only wondered what was inside it. Chicken Soup? Fruit Cocktail? Well, he decided, only one way to find out.

Warren popped the pull tab.

The second he did a cloud of green mist spilled out of the can. As Warren shouted in surprise, the emerald cloud broke apart, transforming into a dozen snakelike tendrils that poured into him through his mouth and nose. The mist was foul tasting, worse than anything Warren scrounged from the garbage. He wanted to cough and sneeze and expel it from his body, but whatever it was, the mist seemed to seize control of his brain and prevent him from doing so. Totally helpless, he could only writhe in terror as the contents of the can emptied into him.

When it was over, Warren wasn't hungry anymore, and he was warm. He felt…wonderful. Better than ever, in fact.

At peace, he fell into a deep slumber.

His dreams were filled with blood and screams.

By morning the storm was over and Warren continued west. He hadn't even gone a mile when he heard a car coming up the road behind him. Warren turned toward the vehicle and held out his thumb with guarded optimism. To his delight, the car slowed down and pulled to the shoulder just ahead of him.

As Warren got into his car, the driver was momentarily startled by the unearthly green glow of Warren's eyes. But it must have been a trick of light, because when the driver blinked, he saw that Warren's eyes were as brown and unremarkable as his own.

"Where you headed?" the driver asked once they got moving. "As far west as you can take me," Warren replied, and began slipping the knife he'd taken from the pantry out of his coat pocket.

The End.

CASE #67544

THE CAN

BY KYLE BAKKE

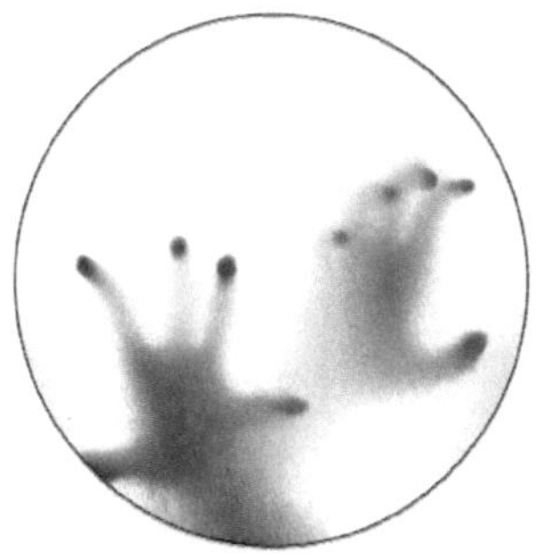

Details not released at this time

Steam by Erik Schechter

When Marissa ran it by Ray, he flashed her these yellow slivers of teeth. Then he coughed a short, nicotine-flecked laugh that trailed off into a wheeze.

"Nah, it wasn't the co-op board," Ray said.

"So why *did* he leave?" Marissa asked, surprised her theory found no traction.

On Monday, the super had quit—not just quit: bolted, didn't even say goodbye. That made it a total of three supers gone since she had moved into her aunt's apartment only two and a half years ago. Now, a turnover rate like that might be normal at McDonald's, but it wasn't for a residential building on the Upper West Side— not even for a gray, sullen one like theirs.

There had to be a logical explanation, Marissa insisted, and barring a better answer from Ray, her money was still on the co-op board.

Why the board? *Because they're petty, nickel-and-diming shits.* They had every opportunity in the world to return The Palandier to its former glory. They could have replaced the dingy peach wallpaper in the hallways, rehung the old grand chandelier in the lobby. (The canopy and wire leads were still in the ceiling; all they needed to do was fix an arm or two and buy a few replacement crystals.) But, instead, they preferred to a wage a vicious war against the widow in B3 all because she kept a parakeet.

So, no, it wasn't hard to imagine the board picking at the supers until they all gave up.

Still, Marissa was willing to hear out Ray. The broken, old gossip usually knew what he was talking about. He had lived in the building for a decade and change—right before the last of the decorative brass lighting fixtures in the hallways were sold off. More than that, he was always puttering around the lobby in his pungent bathrobe. Talking to people. Listening.

"It's the pipes." Ray brushed back a few lonely hairs on his otherwise bald scalp. "The hissing and banging freaks out people. And, eventually, they just up and leave."

Marissa cocked her head and smiled quizzically.

"Seriously? It's just steam, condensation, backed up pipes, whatever," she said. "I'm pretty sure anyone who works as a super understands the concept."

"There's no steam in there. Hasn't been for years," Ray snorted. Then he gave the walls and ceiling a onceover as if he could see the steel pipes running under the ancient plaster, wrapped in their cocoons of asbestos and dead spiders.

"No steam"—Marissa registered the words; they just didn't make any sense. *Is he setting me up?* She scanned his face for a tell.

But there was nothing. No twitch. No slippery ghost of a smile at the corner of his mouth.

"Ray, of course, there's steam. The radiators get super-hot," Marissa said. "Like summertime in hell hot."

"I know. You ain't the only one who feels them. It's just that it's not steam."

Marissa rolled her eyes.

"Ok, fine," Ray said, sighing deeply. "You really want to hear this?"

It happened 17 or 18 years ago, he said, around Christmas time. The boiler in the building exploded, knocking out the electric water heater and killing the super, who was tending to a stuck valve.

The janitor was mopping in the lobby when he heard what sounded like a bomb going off. Pushing through a dark screen of dust in the stairwell, the janitor headed into the basement, where he found the super impaled by a twisted section of boiler. Under the intense heat of the blasted metal, parts of clothing and flesh were peeling away from the man.

"They say it was like watching bacon sizzle in a pan," Ray recounted.

Marissa flinched hard at the detail. "Okay, that was too much," she murmured, but Ray, either not hearing her or intent on poking about every grisly corner of the story, continued.

"So he's screaming in agony—"

"Hey, hey," she jumped in again, this time her voice climbing more than a few decibels. "Seriously, Ray. I have PTSD. Enough with the burning man."

"Oh." Then, after the slightest pause: "Sorry."

"It's OK. You didn't know," she said, pulling her voice back down to conversational level. "Let's just …maybe another time."

***

The radiator in her living room was hissing louder than usual when Marissa got home. She considered the squat, furiously hot metal beast for a moment. The air above the radiator crackled as it belched in high and low notes.

"How is that not steam?" She muttered angrily, then went to the bathroom.

You're fine, she thought as she reached for a bottle in her medicine cabinet.

One Ambien later, she was tucked under her down covers. It's only a Saturday afternoon catnap, Marissa told herself; she wouldn't sleep through dinner again.

***

She forgot how the dream began. But there was a thin, discolored figure—a woman, she realized—sitting stiff, like a soldier, in a plain wooden chair, its back turned to Marissa. The woman never showed her face, and the voice was low and raspy, but Marissa found her familiar all the same.

"Auntie?"

"Marissa, I wish to God you hadn't moved into this place," the figure croaked.

"Why?" she asked.

There was no answer. Just the banging of a steam pipe.

***

"Are you sure about this?" Ray asked, eyeing her cautiously. "Because last time..."

104

"I know," Marissa said. "It just caught me off guard. That's all. Anyway, I can't be running away from a story, right?"

Ray nodded gravely and continued. The boiler had been torn inside out, and the super was writhing on the floor. He lasted maybe ten minutes that way, screaming for his wife Loraine, before, mercifully, going silent.

The fatal accident had been tragic. Harrowing. But in a city caked in inches of dirt and blood, it would have been easily forgotten if not for a problem with the pipes a few years later.

Ray didn't remember the details, but for some reason, the building's boiler had to be turned off, and once the problem was fixed, someone forgot to switch it back on. However, no one noticed the slip-up because everyone in the building was still getting heat.

It was the next super who discovered the oversight when checking a gauge one February snowstorm. He was perfectly fine when he went downstairs. But two hours later, he emerged from the basement pale and listing to one side, hand over his heart, and stuttering about a man stuck in the pipes.

The man, he said, was screaming under the banging metal. News of the bizarre episode quickly reached the co-op board, and they asked the super what he had heard *specifically*. He whispered, "Loraine."

The directors cast dread looks, murmuring to themselves. They knew the name. And they knew what it meant. Indeed, one board member was supposedly so stricken by the super's unsettling report that it seemed as if he was going to be sick right then and there.

But the super wasn't done yet. He also noted that the boiler was off. What did that mean, they asked. It meant that, as far as he could tell, the heat that flooded out of the radiators in all the apartments had nothing to do with steam.

It came from *somewhere else.*

No longer able to contain himself, one board member—the anxious man who had very nearly puked on his shoes—asked the super if he thought the mysterious heat was connected to the ghost.

The super, tired and helpless, couldn't say. But that didn't stop the questions from coming. The fatal boiler accident happened in the winter, the member recalled. Is that why they were getting heat in the right season? And what about the smells; did anyone else notice sulfur coming off the radiators?

The super didn't stay on too long after that, and the co-op board issued orders against anyone touching the boiler. And that's how things were left: a dead metal loop and a howling black-charred seraph in limbo.

***

The story, Marissa had to admit, set her hair on end.

But it's just a story, she reminded herself, and a second-hand one at that. Ray hadn't witnessed any of it himself—he couldn't have: it happened, if it happened at all, years before he even moved into the building.

"You know, you can hear him if you listen carefully," he added. That was supposed to be the clincher, she realized. *Hold your ear close to the radiator, and you'll hear a ghost.* It was no different from when she was in the second grade and the older kids in the cool corduroy jeans told her to play Zeppelin's "Stairway to Heaven" backwards and listen for the satanic message.

Of course, she heard it. She'd been primed for it. But that didn't make it real.

"You can't just turn boilers off," Marissa insisted. "There's got to be city inspections or something."

"Puh-lease," Ray responded, waving his hand, as if the question were a fly that could be shooed away. "If inspections were done by the book, a third of the buildings in this city would be in trouble."

"OK, fine. Say the story is true—" "It *is* true."

"—OK, it's true. They discovered that the ghost of a dead super was heating the pipes. Why didn't they just bring in a priest or something, say a prayer, and free his soul?"

"Because they're saving money on heating oil," he said, shrugging as if to add, *"Sorry, but that's the way the world works."*

Marissa paused to consider Ray's claim. It dovetailed perfectly with her own low opinion of the board, but what about everyone else? Her thoughts turned to the tenants of this dull, decaying box of a middle-class dream: the retirees with arthritic joints, the weary professional couples struggling to keep a toehold in Manhattan— the next of kin with limited options.

"Who else knows this story?" she asked.

"I'd say a good half of the old-timers, even if they won't admit it," Ray said.

"Did my aunt know too?"

Ray nodded.

It was awful, surreal, sickening. All Marissa could see in front of her was a man half consumed by flame, dying in the dark and then, if there was any truth to Ray's morbid tale, lost—lost to the pipes, lost to the building, moving up and dropping down, trapped in a circuit like a shrieking electrical current, while the rest of them kept warm off his pain.

The very idea drained her like leech.

"Well, I got to go. This cigarette won't smoke itself," Ray said with grim determination.

Marissa watched him as he walked away, then turned round herself, and headed to the elevator. On her way up, she tried to reorder herself after the initial shock. She wanted to believe that had been a joke, but Ray held to the story. Plus, she heard the bitterness in his words, and she knew that at least he believed what he had told her.

That sort of conviction is infectious.

***

Ray and Marissa would cross paths in the lobby over the following weeks. They'd exchange clipped hellos by the mailboxes in the lobby, argue a bit about the Knicks and the best way to rebuild the team, but the ghost in the pipes was not brought up again.

Marissa still meditated on it, though. At night especially. Every place has its own sounds—peculiarities that, over time, a resident gets used to, or does not. In her own apartment, the plaster below the crown moldings would creak for unknown reasons, while the refrigerator—growing ever more fickle in its old age—would on occasion sputter out, going quiet for a moment or two, only to growl back to life and continue on like nothing ever happened.

In the dark, those noises and a hundred others played havoc with Marissa's excited brain, conjuring to life the shadows in the corners of her bedroom.

The worst were the banging pipes. Once an annoyance, they now kept her on edge with the thought of waking up to a man's teeth and skin wailing over her bed.

It was a Sunday night, in the middle of January, and in just a few short hours, Marissa's alarm would ring her into five straight days of work. Despite the Ambien and the paid-for promises of modern pharmacology, she still wasn't asleep, her mind having been stirred into action by a barely-there scratching sound.

It's probably a mouse moving between the cupboards in the kitchen, Marissa told herself—nothing unnatural, certainly not a wet, half-formed thing dragging its fingernails along the parquet floor. Yet even as she struggled to keep one fear at bay, her thoughts returned to the super and his miserable fate.

How could they leave a soul trapped like that? It had to be worst sort of sin. She thought about her aunt. The old lady had believed in God, even if she hadn't been the most avid churchgoer. *How could she have gone about her life and her needlework knowing about the pipes?* Marissa hadn't been very good at visiting her aunt after college, especially in those last years, but she always seemed so cheerful when Marissa was a kid.

No, she decided, it was impossible—it was an ugly lie, a dark fantasy harbored by a lonely and bitter old man who was slowly killing himself with cigarettes. Her aunt would've done something about this if it had been real.

Restless, and now angry at herself for ever believing Ray's nonsense, she yanked herself out of bed and went to watch TV in the living room. That's when the radiator kicked in with a *clang-clang-clang*, followed by a drawn-out shushing sound that, for the very first time, made her skin ice over.

The words were working their way up from underneath the hissing.

"Loraine! Loraine! Loraine!"

Marissa stared at the radiator as if it were a cobra ready to strike. Was this really happening? Or could it just be "Stairway to Heaven" doused with Ambien for good measure?

She needed to know. To provoke a response. Real things respond.

Had she thought about it longer, she would have gotten the broom from the kitchen. But, instead, she took a penny from a jar of loose change on the bookshelf and held the coin between a shaking thumb and index finger. Then, backing up as far as she could, she tossed the penny at the radiator.

There was a thin clink, and that's all.

She laughed nervously.

There was no explosion of fire and brimstone, as she had feared, no spectral claw reaching out from the square metal ribs of the radiator to claim her soul. But, as the moments dragged on, Marissa felt a creeping pressure on her skin, and then, finally, she got her answer.

"Bill, get Loraine! Oh, God, Loraine…," a blister-strangled voice gasped between gaseous bursts, and the room began to roar like the ocean.

The air was thick and churning, and Marissa, struggling to breathe, pivoted to the front door only to discover that her feet were now behind her and she was falling forward…

***

The late morning sun danced across the frost on the window as Marissa opened her eyes. She was splayed across the living room floor. Wincing, she traced an angry lump on her temple. She wondered if she had a concussion. It didn't feel like one, but then again, what did she know?

As she staggered to her feet, Marissa wiped her mouth of what she thought was dried drool only to notice dark brown flecks on the back of her hand. *Dirt?* She pushed the specks around with the index finger from the other hand and, forming a suspicion, rubbed her face again; more came off.

"Shit." She stumbled to the bathroom mirror.

It didn't look good. There was the lump—that would need ice later—and her t-shirt was stained with blood. But what scared her most was the crusty black mess around her nostrils. Taking a deep breath, she wiggled her nose—it didn't hurt. *Thank God, thank God,* she thought. *It's not broken. At least there's that.*

Marissa daubed her face with the corner of a warm wet towel, gently removing the dried blood. Then she called the office—yes, she knew it was passed ten-thirty already; no, she wouldn't be coming in; yes, it was serious; it was a head injury, not some rookie hangover; okay, she'd keep them updated.

She threw on a pair of sweatpants and headed over to apartment E8.

"So, you're goldbricking now?" Ray asked as he opened the door. He was wearing his seedy bathrobe and stank like the tailpipe of a taxi. Then he noticed the bump on Marissa's head, and his cigarette smile dropped away. "Jeez, that doesn't look pretty."

"Yeah, I passed out last night, so I'm taking a sick day," she said, looking down for a second, then back up to meet his eyes. "So I guess you know why I'm here, right?"

"It's rough the first time," Ray said. "But, trust me, you can adapt."

"Adapt?"

"You know, get by. Take me, for example. I keep the radio on all winter; it drowns out the voice, and then spring comes by soon enough."

He was trying to being avuncular, she supposed, but she found it reptilian all the same. Waiting for spring? Playing the radio?

They were talking about a man's soul.

"Who's Bill? Was he the janitor who found him?" "Bill?"

"The ghost was calling for him," she said, her arms folded, caressing herself.

"Hmm, that's strange. It's never happened before, as far as I know. The ghost just repeats 'Loraine' over and over," Ray said. "What else did it say to you?"

To me? It was talking to me now? Her eyes began to water.

It started with a cough, or something like it, but quickly turned to full-throttled crying. "Ray, we have to talk to the co-op board," Marissa said, between sobs. "They have to do something about this."

"Hey, there, I know you're upset, but let's not do anything rash," he said, trying to be soothing, but mostly sounding scared himself. "You don't want to stir things up with the co-op board."

"Then I'll just get a priest myself," she said. "They won't even know."

"It won't help because the ghost isn't in your apartment. It's in the pipes. It's all around us. It's the whole building." He waited for that to sink in, then touched her arm and said, "Why don't you get dressed, honey, and go for a walk? Sit at a café and think it over. We can talk again later."

With that, he closed the door on her, and a singed little voice crawled between her ears and whispered, *Marissa, if you stay here, the building will take you too.*

***

Marissa stayed away from her apartment for as long she could. She'd crash with friends for days at a time, telling them that there had been a leak in her bathroom and the slow build-up of rot in the walls meant they would have to be replaced. It would be a messy job, she said, with workmen walking in and out her apartment, supplies everywhere.

She plucked at her cuticle skin as she told them the story. She didn't like to lie; it just added more stress to her already twitchy brain. But what was the alternative? Tell them she was being haunted by a burn victim who talked through the steam pipes? No. They would look at her funny. They would think that this was about Steve again. Poor Marissa, she can't get over her dead college boyfriend, they'd murmur.

This way was better, it offered an escape. For at least a little while.

But this wasn't some haunted inn set on the Scottish moors; this was her life. She couldn't just run away like all those supers. She had a job. She had obligations. She had credit card debt. She would have to return to her apartment eventually.

***

Her heart had started to hammer in her chest the moment she entered the brooding lobby of The Palandier.

Leaning against her door, she whispered to whatever might be listening on the other side, "I just want to get into my apartment. I won't throw any more pennies at the radiator, I promise. So please, let's just be—"

And with that, she eased open the door and smiled wanly.

There was nothing lurking in the living room.

***

Along with her small red suitcase, which served as her traveling closet and laundry bag during her week of house-crashing, Marissa brought home an inflatable air mattress, which she set up in the kitchen, sandwiching it between the dishwasher she rarely used and the gas oven she used even less.

The arrangement looked ridiculous, she had to admit, like one of the tight-fit sleeping cabins on a train, but at least there wasn't a radiator in the kitchen. She could sleep next to the stove while wearing headphones and leave the TV on in the living room, and with any luck, she'd never hear the wailing spirit again.

That's how she planned to outlast winter—to "adapt," as Ray called it.

But each night, one poisonous dream after another set upon her. She'd thrash in her sleep, whimper and lick her lips, but by morning, the terrors would snake away, and Marissa would be left trying to stitch together mere fog and flashes, not sure why she felt so run down.

It continued like this for weeks until one night, a nightmare latched on and didn't let go. It was 1999 again. She was back with Steve, and they were in Vermont for winter break. Chumbawamba was playing on the radio of his beaten-up Ford Fiesta, and everything was beautiful—until it wasn't. Suddenly, they were barreling down an embankment, snow cresting over the windshield in waves.

The car slammed into the pine tree with a deafening crunch, and Marissa was thrown clear of the wreck. But Steve was still inside, pinned under sheets of crumpled metal, when the engine caught fire.

Small flames danced over and around the hood, turning the snow to steam. Soon they would grow in ferocity and consume the rest of the car, leaving Marissa with the same terrible choice she made so long ago. In the dream, she had fractured wrists when she clambered up to the road, so she couldn't possibly have opened Steve's door, even if she had tried. But the real 1999 was different. The car in the dream was different too. When she looked back, it was larger than before, and it wasn't her boyfriend slumped in the driver's seat, but a middle-aged black man in a workman's shirt. He was twisting in pain.

"Loraine! Loraine!" he screamed.

***

When Marissa woke up, slowly, foggily, she saw blood on her pillow. It was another nosebleed—she understood that much, but the splatter, the pattern, it seemed different, enchanting almost. The core stain, deep and dark with rounded borders, looked like a rose, the scattered droplets around it, falling petals. It was romantic in a way.

She craned her head up to the kitchen window and stared out at nothing in particular.

Wake up! The building is taking you.

It was the same voice that talked to her outside Ray's door.

Listen, my beautiful Marissa, Steve is gone. It was a terrible thing. But you were scared, and you weren't thinking right, and there's nothing to be done about it now. So why are you still here? Do you hate yourself so much that you're willing to die?

Did she?

"No," Marissa said weakly, still looking out the window. "I want to live," she told the voice—that other voice, the one she hoped was her aunt's.

***

She'd do it. She'd sell her New York co-op apartment, her terrible inn on the moors. Finding the buyer would be the easy part. Getting the board's blessing would take time.

In the meantime, she would just have to be patient. With any luck, she'd be able to move out by spring. Once again, she'd survive.

***

Human skin scalds at 140 degrees Fahrenheit; all it takes is three seconds. But at what temperature does a psyche burn? How much terror can one person take? How long?

Marissa had changed so much over the winter that the other tenants would shrink from her in the hall. Having quit her job, she seemed oddly listless now. She'd walk around in mismatched clothes, with stained tissues stuck up her nose and bandages wrapped around her hands.

She knew they were gossiping about her, but she really only listened to two voices now, and one was fading away.

"Hey, what's up with the mummy woman?" the doorman of the neighboring building asked Ray while the two were standing outside under the sun.

"Who?"

"The one with the bandages and the *real* slow walk."

"Oh, her? It's hard to say, man. Some people just snap," Ray answered, taking a drag on a cigarette, then shaking his head sympathetically.

Four stories up, Marissa was kneeling before the radiator in her bedroom, her palms pressed against the cast iron. Outside, it was spring, but here it was still winter, and the heat was on, rising in the air with the smell of burned skin.

"Loraine! Loraine!" the voice in the pipes cried. "Oh, Lord Jesus Christ!"

"Shhh, baby. It's okay," she cooed into the metal. "I'm here. I won't leave you this time."

The End.

CASE #: 78577

STEAM

BY ERIK SCHECHTER

E.J. Schechter is a brand-spanking new author. He lives in Brooklyn, New York, with his cat Princess Shwarma, Puffball of Death, and a tangle of houseplants. He does much of his writing at night, in Lower East Side bars.

He can be reached at ejs1776@ hotmail.com.

CASE #: 98815

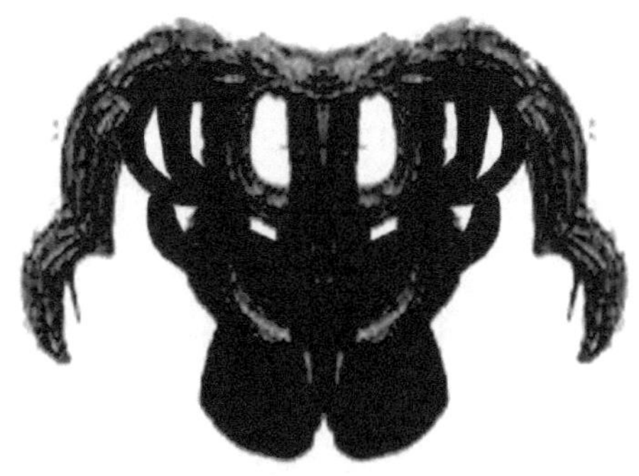

Hangtown by Alex Rezdan

Silence. For as long as he could remember, there was nothing but silence. Nothingness. Oblivion. If this was hell, then he had it worse than he would have ever thought possible. For him, there was no difference between 'deaf' and 'dead,' except that the former would have him wishing for the latter.

But all of that changed with a single turn of a knob; a click of the radio dial. Suddenly, music pierced through the air. The irregular thump of the speaker became his heartbeat and now he was able to see and hear everything around him.

A man with vaguely familiar features peered at the radio counter. He turned a knob to cycle through the frequencies in search of a station playing the music he liked but only found static on all but one, an old-time, wild west saloon station. It was fused deep within the soul of the radio itself, and it felt like taking a fresh breath of air after staying underwater five seconds longer than the longest you can hold your breath.

"That music sounds as old as the radio," said a young boy standing next to the man. He lost interest and plopped onto the couch, raising his iPad up to his face.

"It's probably a lot older than the radio, actually," said the man. He seemed unsure of the music selection at first, but then smiled and accepted it, nodding his head along with the rhythm.

A woman stepped into the room with a small child following close behind.

"Oh? Is it break time already?" she said.

The man smiled and stood up straight from crouching. "Well howdy tharr, Miss Rachel," he said, imitating a cowboy accent. He took her hand and kissed her knuckles. "I reckon now's as good a time as any ta eat some grub. Whadd'ya say?"

The small boy giggled from behind his mother. "Why are you talking like that, Andy?"

Andrew placed his hands on his hips and looked at the boy. "Now is that the young Thomas Chambers I see before me? Come here." He picked the boy up into the air and stepped towards the kitchen. "A little gunslinger like yourself could go for some pasghetti right now, don't ya think?"

"It's SPA-ghetti," said Thomas, giggling again.

"Well now, talent AND brains. Ain't that somethin'," said Andrew.

"Well, I suppose I am starting to feel hungry," said Rachel. "We can finish unpacking tomorrow."

"Yeehaw," said Andrew. He put Thomas down. "Why don't you go play with Sam over there for a while?"

"Yeehaw," repeated Thomas as he ran and jumped next to the preteen on the couch.

"What's with the saloon theme?" asked Rachel.

"Sam found that old radio collecting dust in his new closet. Seems like maybe the previous owners never used it and just forgot about it." Andrew placed a pot on the sink and half-filled it with water. "I'm surprised it still works, to be honest. Could only pick up this station, though." He set the pot on the stove, covered it with a lid, and lit the flame.

"I'm surprised there's a station even playing this music," said Rachel. She sidled up behind Andrew, placing her arms around his waist and her head against his back. "I have some big news for you."

"Really? What's up?"

She bit her lower lip and reached one hand to the pregnancy test stick in her pocket. Taking a deep breath, she began to slide it out when she was interrupted.

"Ewww," screamed Sam. "Go to the bathroom, sicko!"

The two adults turned their attention to the two boys. Thomas was covering his mouth with one hand and holding his stomach with the other. A pool of vomit decorated the carpet and some of the couch in front of him. He looked like he might throw up again at any second.

"You're so gross," said Sam. "Get the hell away from me." Rachel pushed the pregnancy stick back into her pocket and

rushed over. "Oh, honey. Come with me. Let's get you cleaned up." She led Thomas away to the bathroom down the hall.

Andrew wet a rag and did his best to clean the carpet and couch. "Take it easy on him," he said to Sam. "He's only five years old."

"Do we really have to live with them from now on?" said Sam.

"Yes, so be nice. He's going to be your little brother pretty soon."

"Couldn't you have picked someone with a better kid?"

He's too weak. You're the better choice.

The distorted voice crackled from the speaker over the music on the radio. It sounded sinister and threatening, not like any radio announcer Sam had ever heard before. He turned to his dad, who was looking back at him disapprovingly.

"You know what," said Andrew. "Put the iPad away and come help me set the table for dinner."

His father didn't seem to react to the menacing voice. Was Sam hearing things? Or was it a normal part of the program? This was a pretty weird station, he thought.

Andrew took the tablet away from his son and put it on the desk next to the radio. "Come on," he said. "You want someone with a better kid, then we might as well start with ourselves."

Yes. Let's start with you.

Sam looked at the radio. There was definitely something strange about it. He rose to his feet and suddenly felt dizzy. The floor felt off-balance and askew, and his father's face warped as if he was looking at him through bent glass. He quickly sat back down and raised a hand to his forehead.

"What's wrong?" asked Andrew.

Don't fight it.

"I don't know," said Sam. "I just got really dizzy all of a sudden." "Probably 'cause you don't exercise enough. You're always sitting on a couch with your face in front of a screen. Not to mention all the crap you eat."

Let's try again.

Andrew walked to the kitchen and bent down to open a cardboard box labeled "Dishes and Silverware." He took out some ceramic plates and utensils and placed them on the counter next to the sink.

"I'm going to give these a quick rinse," he said, "and then I want you to place them on the table in front of each seat."

He turned the knob for the water, and in that exact moment, the music exploded into cacophonous ricochets in Sam's head. It lasted only a fraction of a second, but when it stopped, he felt a strange detachment from his body. Everything seemed normal, but it was as if he was now a passenger in his own body.

Andrew turned the water off and dried the wet plate with a towel. He held it out towards Sam. "Are you really going to make me repeat myself?"

Sam found himself rising to his feet again. His body walked to the kitchen and took the plate from his father. Even though he could still feel and see everything normally, the sensation was weird, as if his brain was on autopilot. He set the plate on the edge of the table and walked back towards his father. His hand rummaged through the utensils and pulled out a sharp steak knife.

Andrew glanced at his son. "We aren't going to need that one, actually," he said. "You can just throw it back in the box for now." He returned his attention to drying the next plate.

Sam willed his body to toss the knife into the cardboard box, but it wouldn't move. Not even his eyes obeyed his commands. His hand clutched the knife and raised it above his head. This definitely wasn't autopilot, Sam thought. Something has taken over control of his body. Positioning himself behind his father's back, Sam realized what was about to happen. A sinister laugh echoed in his mind right before his hand slammed the knife down with all the strength his twelve-year-old body could muster.

Andrew cried out in pain. The plate fell from his hands and broke into pieces in the sink. His legs buckled, and he had to grab the edge of the counter to keep from falling over. He sunk to his knees and desperately tried to grab at the knife jutting out of his back, but it was out of his reach.

Rachel ran in from the hallway. "What happened?"

Andrew gritted his teeth together and grunted through the pain. "My… fucking… back!"

"Oh, my God." Rachel could not make sense of how something like that could have occurred. "Hang on. I'll call for some help." She rushed over to her purse.

Sam was horrified, but he could feel his lips turn up into a smile. His father turned around to look at him and mouthed the word "Why?" Sam had no idea why he had done what he just did. It didn't make any sense. It was not him. Something made him do it.

That something could feel the presence of anger and rage radiating from Andrew's body. It had just enough control over Sam, but it wanted more. With that knife wound, it would have no problem at all taking over Andrew's body. It left Sam and danced around the knife's edge, tickling the bleeding wound. It offered the promise of relief, of the pain going away, and as it predicted, Andrew fully embraced the pleasing sensation.

Sam, now in complete control, rushed to his father's side. "I'm so sorry," said Sam. "I don't know what happened. I couldn't control myself."

He grabbed the knife handle in an attempt to pull it out.

"Sam, no," said Rachel, rushing back over to the two of them. "Leave it alone."

She raised her phone up above her head, waving it around and frantically hoping for a signal.

"Ugh," she said, exasperated. "There's no service here." "Get it out of me," said Andrew. Sam reached for the knife again.

"Stop," said Rachel. "You might hurt him even more." "Well what can I do?" said Sam. "I want to help."

"Just stay with Daddy while I try to get through to the hospital." Rachel moved away from the scene. "I'm just going to be out on the balcony, okay? Stay right there."

"I'm so sorry," said Sam to his father again.

"Oh, you will be," said Andrew, slowly rising and steadying himself. He flexed his hands. "Yeah, this is much better."

"Dad?"

Andrew punched his son square against his jaw, sending him straight down to the floor. His little body offered no resistance. Andrew laughed and kicked him hard against his ribs.

"Andrew," screamed Rachel. "Stop. What are you doing?" But Andrew did not stop. He grabbed a fistful of Sam's hair and pulled him back up to his feet. With his other hand, he slapped him across the face with the back of his hand. Rachel grabbed Andrew's arm and again yelled at him to stop, but he simply shrugged her away and hit Sam again.

"I'm not finished yet," growled Andrew and pulled his hand back for another punch when suddenly the pain returned to his back.

The spirit that had taken over his body now returned to the knife's edge and completely out of the body as Rachel pulled the knife out of Andrew's back. With nothing to grasp onto, the spirit floated helplessly in the air. Vibrations pierced the air and served as a bridge for him to latch onto. It lead him back to the radio where the old-west music was still playing as loud as before. Here, it could refresh and rejuvenate its energy. It would go after the meddling bitch next.

Rachel examined Sam's bruised face. "Hang on, Sam. I'm going to get help, okay? Everything will be okay. It'll be okay."

She repeated the words 'it'll be okay' over and over like a mantra to keep her wits about her.

"Mom?" said Thomas, suddenly appearing from the hallway. "Why is everyone fighting?"

"Oh, Tommy," she said and hugged her son. "It's okay, honey. Go sit on the couch for now." She grabbed the iPad and handed it to the boy. "Play a game while Mommy makes a phone call."

She turned the volume knob on the radio, but the volume remained the same no matter how far to each side she turned it. She tried changing the frequency, but the same music was playing across the entire radio band. Her hand followed the cord and pulled it out of the wall socket, but even with no energy, the radio continued playing the saloon music uninterrupted.

"What the hell..." she said.

Deciding there was no time to figure it out now, she walked over to the sliding glass door leading to the balcony, but no matter how hard she pulled, the door would not budge. She braced her back against the wall and used her foot to push, but it didn't slide even a fraction of a centimeter.

"Dammit," she screamed. Noticing Thomas's concerned face, she put on a smile for him and said, "Just stay right there, baby. Mommy will be right back."

She trudged over to the main bedroom and tried to open the window, but it too was impossibly stuck. She banged against the glass to no avail. She held the phone against the glass hoping for some service to bleed through, but it was no use.

As she looked at the smartphone screen, her vision began to distort. The display seemed to slowly lift from the phone to her face, while at the same time, the phone and her hand seemed to sink deeper along with the floor. She looked away and out the window, but this made the effect even worse, and a strong sense of vertigo overtook her. Her free hand grasped the frame to regain her balance, but the room began to rotate like a boat about to drop down a waterfall, and she felt something push her against the glass. It wasn't the feeling of gravity doing its job, but rather like something was intentionally toying with the physics in her mind.

She pushed herself from the window and landed on the bed. The room returned to its normal orientation and down became down again, but as she looked around the room, it seemed bigger than before. The walls expanded and slipped away from the bed, which had now become the center of the room, slowly at first but exponentially increasing until it seemed like there was nothing in every direction except for the music echoing from down the hall.

That music, she thought, is the epitome of evil. Never had she felt more sure that death itself was mocking her, having one last laugh at her expense before casting its scythe down on her neck. She clenched her eyes shut and let the music lead her where it willed.

"Mom," Thomas shouted from the oblivion.

His voice was a welcome addition over the madness of the music. She tried to latch on to his voice.

"Thomas?"

"Mom, come quick," the little voice said. "Hurry."

Rachel opened her eyes. The room was back to normal. Gravity was operating the way she had always experienced it, and her vision seemed to be back to the way it always was. She took a deep breath and slid herself off of the bed.

Upon returning to the main room, she saw Andrew rummaging through a box in the kitchen. The two boys were on the couch.

They looked frightened of what was happening. Sam held a hand to his face where he had been punched.

"Ah, there we are," said Andrew in another wild west type of accent.

He pulled a bottle of whiskey out of the box and set it next to a glass on the counter. He noticed Rachel standing in the arch of the hallway but didn't seem to care. Instead, he cracked open the seal and poured himself a generous ounce, then slammed it down his throat and back to the counter with a bang.

"Ahhh," he breathed out, satisfied. "Ain't no Old Overholt, I'll tell ya that, but damn fine, nonetheless."

"Andrew," said Rachel. "You shouldn't be moving around right now."

Andrew ignored her. He placed three fingers against the glass and poured the liquor until it reached the top of his index finger. Raising the glass to his mouth once more, he poured most of it in and savored the taste before chugging it down.

"Andrew," Rachel repeated. "Maybe you should sit down." "Woman," he snapped. "Maybe you should shut yer mouth." He looked her up and down and smacked his lips together followed by a slow shake of the head.

"Mmmm," he said. "I am gonna have fun with you."

He sauntered over to her and took her hair in his empty hand, lifting it to his nostrils and breathing in her smell. She tried to shy away, but he gripped her hair firmly and held her in place. The struggle caused him to spill some of his drink.

"Woman," he said. "Don't you ever get between a man and his bourbon."

"Dad," said Sam from the couch, "you're bleeding all over the carpet."

Closing his eyes, Andrew lifted his head to the ceiling as if asking God to give him patience. He downed what remained of the liquor and held the glass in front of his face. Breathing out, he let the stench of alcohol wash over Rachel's face and released his grip on her hair.

"And whose goddamn fault is that," he said in a rising crescendo climaxing with him chucking the glass at Sam's head.

The glass exploded right above Thomas's head. The two boys flinched and screamed instinctively. Part of their faces and arms got scratched trying to avoid the shattering glass.

"What the hell has gotten into you?" said Rachel.

"I know something that's gonna get into you," said Andrew as he grabbed his crotch. He laughed and reached for her hair again, but he did not get the chance to grab it this time.

Rachel's foot came up swiftly and connected with his groin. Andrew yelped out in pain and keeled over onto the floor, smacking his head as he went down. A high-pitched whine escaped from his vocal cords.

Rachel rushed over to the two boys.

"Are you two okay?" she said. "Let me see where you got cut." "We're fine," said Sam. "But something isn't right here. I don't think that's my dad."

"What?" she said, struggling to hear his words.

The music from the radio increased its volume dramatically. It was deafening and maddening. Rachel again fiddled with the knobs, trying everything she could think of to turn it off, but nothing worked. In a last-ditch effort, she threw it against the glass door leading to the balcony. It bounced off and landed on the floor unharmed.

Again, she braced her back against the wall and used her feet in an attempt to get the door open. She screamed with each kick, but it still would not budge. She picked up the radio again and slammed it as hard as she could against the glass. Nothing happened except that it bounced out of her grasp and back to the floor, still unharmed.

Giving up, she placed her palms on the glass and rested her forehead against the sliding door. She noticed the light coming from the building beside theirs. The room was on the same floor, and inside, a middle-aged couple could be seen watching TV in their apartment.

"Sam," said Rachel, not taking her eyes away from the neighbors. "Go to the light switch and turn it off and on over and over again. Don't stop until I tell you."

Sam did not understand why he was being asked to do that.

He looked quizzically at Rachel and remained seated on the couch.

"There's something coming from the radio," he said. "It won't let us leave."

"Sam, please," said Rachel. "Just do what I say."

Sam rose from the couch and walked over to the light switch next to the entrance door. He glanced at his father, who was still on the floor holding his groin and rocking back and forth. His father may have a short temper sometimes, but he would never do anything to harm anyone. Whatever it was that punched him, it wasn't his dad. Sam knew that for sure. It was the same thing that made him stab the knife into his back. And it all started with that voice from the radio.

He flicked the light off and saw the light from the next building that Rachel must have noticed. Now he understood. Maybe they could still call for help without needing to use the phone. He flicked the light back on again. Would this really be enough to get someone's attention?

"You need to do it faster," said Rachel.

She remained focused on the couple watching TV. When the light came back on, her reflection appeared in the glass. It disappeared with the flick of the switch, then reappeared, again and again. The couple did not so much as give one curious look towards their apartment.

"Do it as fast as you can," she said.

"Mom, look out," Thomas screamed.

The light came back on. This time, Andrew's reflection appeared right behind Rachel's in the glass. He smiled and placed his hand on the back of her head, then slammed it against the glass. The door cracked with the impact. Rachel stumbled backwards and fell to the floor.

Andrew looked at the cracked glass and whistled. "Boy, you have a hard head." He laughed.

Sam ran to them and stood between him and Rachel.

"Leave my dad alone," he said.

Andrew placed a hand on his shoulder and easily tossed him towards the couch. He let out an impatient sigh and gave the kids a disdainful look.

"Why are you doing this?" asked Rachel, propping herself on her elbows.

"Why?" said Andrew. He looked away from the kids at Rachel. "Your husband knows the score, ma'am. Thinks he can ride with Quickdraw and his gang, doing whatever it is they please, and get away scot free? Thinks he can murder my whole family and bury me alive without any consequences? Uh-uh. No way."

"Quickdraw? What are you talking about?"

"Now I know you ain't had nothing to do with what Frankie did, but he didn't much care about my family's innocence, so it's only fair I show him the same amount of respect, don't you think? Now this whole family's gotta pay the price." He laughed. "Funny I'll be using Frankie's own body to kill his family, though. Poetic justice, wouldn't you say? The devil sure does have a twisted sense of humor."

"Who's Frankie?"

Andrew's face tightened. "Now don't play dumb. Your husband. Franklin Malone. The soon-to-be dead man once I kill off this body. That is, after I'm done with you and your young ones here."

"Andrew, please. This stupid game stopped being funny a long time ago."

"That's not my dad," said Sam. "Something is controlling him. There's some kind of ghost that came from the radio."

"Smart kid," said Andrew. "Allow me to introduce myself. My name is Richard Jackson, and I'll be your executioner tonight."

"You guys have a really sick sense of humor," said Rachel. "Really, this has gone way too far."

Andrew kicked Rachel against her ribs. She fell back to the floor. "Mom," cried Thomas. He tried to go to her, but Sam held him back.

"This ain't no game," said Andrew. "But anyway, you're right. Let's stop playing around and get to the point." He reached for her hair and pulled her up to her feet.

"Please," said Rachel, realizing now that all of this was real. "We don't know any Franklin Malone. You've got the wrong family."

"Nice try," said Andrew and punched her stomach.

Rachel pushed herself away, scratching and slapping Andrew to get him to release his grip. She hugged her stomach and took quick breaths, hoping the hit was not strong enough to hurt her unborn baby. She raised her hand when Andrew took a step towards her.

"I'm telling you the truth," she said. "We're not who you think we are."

Andrew stopped and turned around. He looked at his cracked reflection in the glass door and touched his face.

"Huh," he said. He looked around the room. "What is this place? This don't look like no house I've ever seen before." He stepped towards the glass door and looked at the view from the balcony. He quickly took a step back when he realized how high up they were. "Holy! Where the hell am I? This ain't Hangtown."

"We're in Placerville. In California."

"Placerville…? Ain't no one call it that. How long have I been out? What year is it now?"

"It's 2015."

"Say again…?" Andrew could not believe it.

This time, it was he who noticed a new reflection in the glass with no time to react or turn around. Sam held the radio above his head and slammed it down onto Andrew's back at the precise spot where the knife wound was located. He bounced off the glass and collapsed to the floor in terrible pain.

Rachel pulled Sam back and pushed both him and Thomas behind her. She grabbed the knife from before and held it out in front of her, pointing it directly at Andrew.

Holding his back, he got back to his feet and laughed. "Hurts like a motherfucker," he said, "but you're only hurting your dad in the long run. I was almost willing to listen to reason and leave you good folks alone, but now I see you're not really good folks at all." "Please just leave us alone," said Rachel. "We haven't done anything to deserve this."

"Deserve?" Andrew spat on the ground. "Let me tell you something about deserve. I work all day and all night to give my family a decent living, and one day I stumble across some gold left behind the back of the saloon. Now, I'm a decent man, I know it belongs to someone, so I resolve to turn it in to the sheriff's first thing in the morning, but Quickdraw and a bunch of his thugs follow me home and demand that I give it to them. Well, I obliged, but did they leave us alone? No, ma'am. They wanted more. And once they were finished taking everything they wanted, Frankie got it in his head that he wanted to rape my wife right in front of me and my baby boy. I tried to defend her, but they overpowered me. Next thing I know, I wake up as they're digging a hole to bury us in. My wife and my kid, both dead at my side. It was at that moment that I swore revenge and signed a deal with the devil to avenge my family by killing that whole gang, especially Frankie Malone."

Andrew shook his head. "Deserve… That word has no place in reality. This world will throw everything it has at you, and you can either take a beating and die or fight back and give it everything you've got. Well, I'm going to fight back. If I can't get my revenge, then I'm going to take my second chance at life."

At that moment, Sam ran from behind Rachel's back and straight towards Andrew. Andrew moved to the side to avoid him, but Sam had another target in mind. He jumped as high as he could and smashed his feet straight down onto the radio, breaking it in half. He continued to stomp on it until the music finally stopped, then gave it one last bash of the heel for good measure. He looked up at his father with hope to see if his plan to kill the spirit worked.

Andrew laughed. "Don't exert yourself, kid. What did you think would happen? You destroy that music box and everything goes back to normal? Let me tell you a secret. I haven't always lived inside of that. I can latch on to anything. But now, I kind of like having a body. I think I'm going to stay right where I am."

His body suddenly dropped to the floor. Rachel stood over him with the knife in her hand. She had smashed the butt of the handle on the back of his head with as much force as she could muster, hoping it would be enough to incapacitate him without killing him.

"Help me tie him up," she said to Sam.

***

Richard Jackson opened his eyes and saw boots walking around on the dirt, kicking up dust with every step. His entire body ached. He rolled his head to the side and saw a pair of tiny hands lying limply on the ground. Squinting against the sun, he recognized the body they belonged to as his son.

"Percey?" he said. "Hey, Percey, are you all right?" The body lay motionless.

"Lookie here," said a voice. "He's still alive."

"I told you he weren't dead," said a different voice.

"Hey, keep diggin'," said a third.

Spurs clinked against the boots that approached into Richard's view. A tall, slender silhouette wearing a cowboy hat blocked out the sun. The shadow man spat tobacco on the boy's corpse.

"You son of a bitch," screamed Richard. He squirmed to try to break free from the rope tied around his wrists. "I'm going to kill you."

The shadow lifted his foot and slammed it down onto Richard's shoulder. The spur dug into his collarbone, breaking the skin.

"You best be shuttin' that mouth a yer's," said the second voice from before. "Else Quickdraw'll shut it fer good."

With Quickdraw blocking the sun, Richard was now able to get a good look at the men digging. He recognized the one that just spoke as the man who went after his wife right before he lost consciousness.

"What did you do to Mellie?" said Richard. "Answer me, you son of a bitch."

The shadow bent down and gripped Richard by the chin, turning his face for him to get a good look. A chiseled face with a few days' stubble grinned right at him. Two eyes peered on with absolutely no sympathy. The eyes of a person killing for the pure enjoyment of it. The eyes that could only belong to no animal other than a human being.

"Is that the only insult you know?" said Quickdraw. His voice was soft and enunciated perfectly, like that of a college-aged schoolboy. He looked up at his partner. "Hey, Frankie, looks like we're both sons of bitches."

"That don't sound right," said Frankie.

"No, it don't," said Quickdraw with a smile.

"Frankie," said Richard. "He's the one that attacked my wife."

"Attacked, raped, and killed," said Quickdraw.

Richard backed his head away out of Quickdraw's grip and spat in his face. Quickdraw kept his composure. The others stopped digging.

Wiping the spit away with his jacket sleeve, Quickdraw said, "Good news, boys. We only need to dig one grave." He yanked Richard to his feet and pushed him to the hole. "Say hello to your wife." Quickdraw kicked him into the open pit.

Richard landed on his shoulder and felt the bones snap out of place. His wife's body did nothing to cushion the fall. Her limp body gave no reaction to the impact, confirming that she was no longer alive. He scooted himself up to see her face. It was mangled and bruised beyond repair.

"Oh, Mellie," said Richard. "God... Mellie, I'm sorry." Quickdraw snapped his fingers. "Yoohoo."

Richard looked up just in time for Percey to land right on his chest. He felt the wind get knocked out of him and struggled to breathe.

"Isn't that sweet?" said Quickdraw. "The whole family. Together forever." He patted his comrade on the back. "Franklin Malone, I do believe the honor is yours."

"What? All by myself?" said Frankie.

"You pick 'em, you dig 'em," said Quickdraw and turned around to leave.

The others sneered and poked fun at Frankie, then followed behind their leader.

"Aw, hell," said Frankie. He picked up a shovel and pitched some dirt into the grave.

The dirt hit Richard in the face. Spitting it out of his mouth, he said, "Wait. Just wait a minute. There's no need to do this."

"I can't hear no dead men talk," said Frankie and threw a bigger clump of dirt. He had no intention of stopping.

"You goddamn son of a bitch. You better pray I don't get out of here, because I'll be comin' for ya."

"Yeah, yeah. I'm a son of a bitch." He shoveled in a patch of dirt. "He's a son of a bitch." Again, he threw more in. "You're a son of a bitch." More dirt. "We're all sons of bitches."

Quicker than he would have imagined, the sounds were drowned out when the next patch of dirt covered him up completely. The only sensation he could feel was the impact of new dirt arriving on top and increasing the pressure around him until there was nothing left.

***

Andrew opened his eyes to the flickering of the light. Sam stood near the door, flipping the light switch off and on as quickly as he could. Thomas and Rachel pounded against the sliding balcony door and shouted to try to get the neighbors' attention. It was no use.

Andrew sat on a chair with his hands tied behind his back. He tried to slip out of the rope, but it was tied too tight. The throbbing on the back of his head prevented him from thinking clearly.

"Sam," he said.

Everyone stopped what they were doing and looked at him. "Guys," he continued, "I'm all right now. Whatever was controlling me before, it's gone now."

They looked at each other. Rachel stepped close to him. "Really," said Andrew. "You can untie me."

"I think," said Rachel, "that while we figure this out, for your own safety, it'll probably be better if you stay right here."

"Honey, please. At least loosen it up a bit. My hands are going numb."

Rachel hesitated for a moment. "Sorry," she said.

"Babe, it's okay. It's me in control now."

"I believe you. I just… can't. I'm sorry."

"You," said Andrew. "Dammit. You fucking bitch. I'm going to fucking kill you. I'm going to make you watch me kill your kids and then I'm going to fuck you before fucking killing you."

Thomas clasped his hands over his ears and shut his eyes. "Stop," he yelled. "Stop being so mad."

Rachel clutched him in her arms. "That's not Andy, baby. Don't worry. Everything will be okay."

"Sam," said Andrew. "Come over here and untie your father." Sam lowered his eyes.

Andrew struggled against the ropes, trying to force them to rip free.

"I know my dad is still in there somewhere," said Sam. "When it took over my body, I was still able to see everything going on." "Andrew," said Rachel. "Andrew, if you're still in there, you have to fight that thing. Fight back. Take control." Andrew laughed.

"We believe in you," said Rachel.

"Well, that's nice," said Andrew. "Too bad it don't work that way, darlin'. As long as I'm here, he ain't."

"What do you want from us?" said Rachel. "Everyone you want to get revenge on died a long time ago. We have nothing to do with what happened to you."

"Maybe. Maybe not. Honestly, though, I don't really care about revenge anymore. All I want is a new life. I don't ever want to go back to nothingness again."

"You can have that. Just please leave us in peace."

Andrew shook his head. "You don't get it. I'm not leaving this body. It's mine now."

There was a knock on the door. "Police," said a voice. "Open up."

Andrew looked shocked. "What the hell?" He tried to focus but the throbbing in his head just intensified.

"Your power doesn't work anymore," said Sam. "We still can't open the doors, but we can get service on our phones now."

"What in the hell is a phone?" said Andrew.

The knock was louder this time.

"Help," screamed Sam at the door. "The door's stuck. We can't get it open."

Muffled voices talked back and forth through the door, then the original voice returned louder and said, "Stand back. We're going to kick it open."

Sam moved away from the door while the police counted down from three and kicked the door into the room. A piece of the door frame burst out of the wall. Two police officers stepped into the room and assessed the situation. They looked from Andrew to the other three huddled together near the cracked sliding door.

"What's going on here?" said Rodriguez, the cop who had been talking through the door.

"Oh, thank God, officer," said Andrew. "They attacked me and tied me up. You've gotta help me."

"Liar," cried Thomas.

"No way," said Sam. "That thing attacked us first."

"Ma'am," said Rodriguez. "You want to tell us what happened?" Rachel hesitated a moment. A tear rolled down her cheek. "He threatened to kill us. He kept hitting Sam," she placed a hand on Sam's shoulder, "so I had no choice but to stop him. He kept fighting back so I hit him hard on the head and tied him up while he was unconscious."

"But that's not my dad," said Sam.

Rachel put pressure on his shoulder and shook her head. "We can explain all that later, dear."

"Wow," said Andrew. "They'll say anything to blame me. I'm the victim here, officers. I'm the one that's hurt here."

"The kid looks pretty banged up to me," said Miller, the other cop.

"That woman sure can inflict some damage," said Andrew. "Please," said Rachel. "Is there any way you can lock him away somewhere safe? He needs a place to calm down." "I don't look calm to you?"

Rodriguez nodded his head at Miller, who then proceeded to untie the knots around Andrew's wrists. Andrew eyed the gun on his hip.

"Damn, you really tied these tight," said Miller before finally releasing the tension and freeing Andrew's hands.

Immediately, Andrew reached for the gun. He pushed Miller away and slipped the pistol out of the holster, only to turn around straight into Rodriguez's taser. The electricity coursed throughout his entire body and sent it straight down to the floor.

Richard Jackson found himself floating freely in the air again. The body that was his previous host was now too weak to hold onto. He lunged his spirit straight towards Rachel. He would show that bitch who's in control by using her body to kill the kids. This time, he would be more subtle about it. He entered into her body and prepared to take control, but found himself instead in another state of darkness. It was like before, when he was trapped in the radio, except this time, it felt different. He had a heartbeat, but that was about all he could feel. He tried to move, but there was nothing else. His spirit latched on and refused to leave this body. The more he struggled, the stronger the bond became.

The three of them watched as the two police officers put handcuffs on Andrew and picked him up to his feet. He looked confused and relieved, and too weak to say or do anything other than stumble in the direction the cops lead him.

Rachel felt an uneasiness in her stomach. Placing her hand on her belly, she sat down and thought of her baby, hoping that everything was okay.

The End.

CASE #98815

HANGTOWN
BY ALEX REZDAN

Alex Rezdan is an American writer currently living in Berlin, although he still fondly reminisces about his time living in Vietnam and Indonesia. His short stories have previously appeared in Popshot, Literally Stories, and Fabula Argentea. When not traveling to new countries or procrastinating with classical piano, Alex likes to hang out in cemeteries and daydream about the lives of the people who have found their final resting place. He hopes to finish rewriting his novel and see it on a bookshelf before finding his own final permanent address.

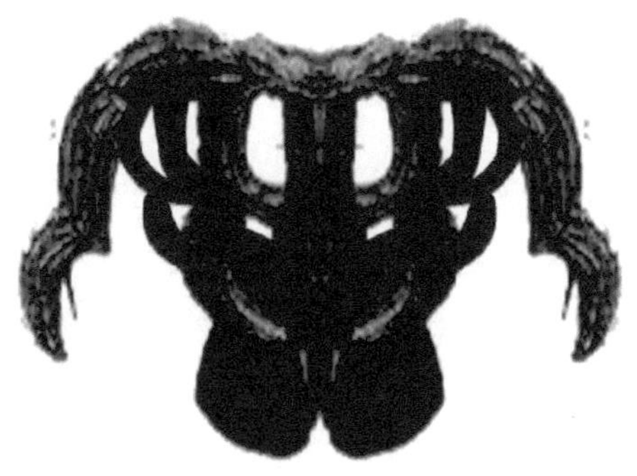

Mr. Scary by Joseph Danoski

Black and desolate at the edge of town,

In an abandoned cemetery;

Shrouded in mystery, Stands the

strange old tree That the kids call

Mr. Scary.

It's said that this specter for centuries fed Upon

the gruesome nourishment

And dregs of the dead;

Like a nightmare dark in the light of day — Like a golem

growing from the graveyard clay.

See its twisted limbs against the twilight,

Where the night birds come to roost;

And dark figures in hoods

From the haunted woods

Gather like Druids to draw from its roots.

Some say, like a mandrake, you secretly sprang From

the grave of a man

Who was innocently hanged;

With a monstrous shape and a knothole face— With the

rotten soul of this unholy place.

Dreaded tree of life in the dead of night—
Silhouette against the moon;

In the shadows of doom

And your midnight gloom,

Standing like ruins through each afternoon.

CASE #82631
MR. SCARY
BY JOSEPH DANOSKI

Joseph V. Danoski lives happily on the "plains of his imagination" in the White Mountains of New Hampshire. He published his first book of poems, Shock Waves: Letters from the Edge, back in 1987, under his infamous pen name, Jonathan Konrad. This book is still being sold in local bookstores, and has been reviewed favorably a number of times.

Through the years, Joseph has had quite a few of his poems published in the city's newspaper, The Berlin Reporter, where for a time he had a byline in its poetry corner. In 1997 he was asked by the Chamber of commerce to write something appropriate for the Berlin Centennial Celebration. After researching the history of the area and the paper-making industry, he wrote a poem titled, The City Built from Trees, which he was subsequently invited to read at City Hall.

Joseph is a writer of letters and essays on diverse subjects, with strong opinions on many topics; but first and foremost, a poet of horror, science fiction and fantasy. His other activities include playing music, gardening, and stargazing. Recent publications include Penny Dreadful, Psychopoetica (U.K.) Hadrosaur Tales, The Quest (India) Black Petals, Yellow Mama, and The Horror Zine.

Email: Dojonaki@Netscape.Net

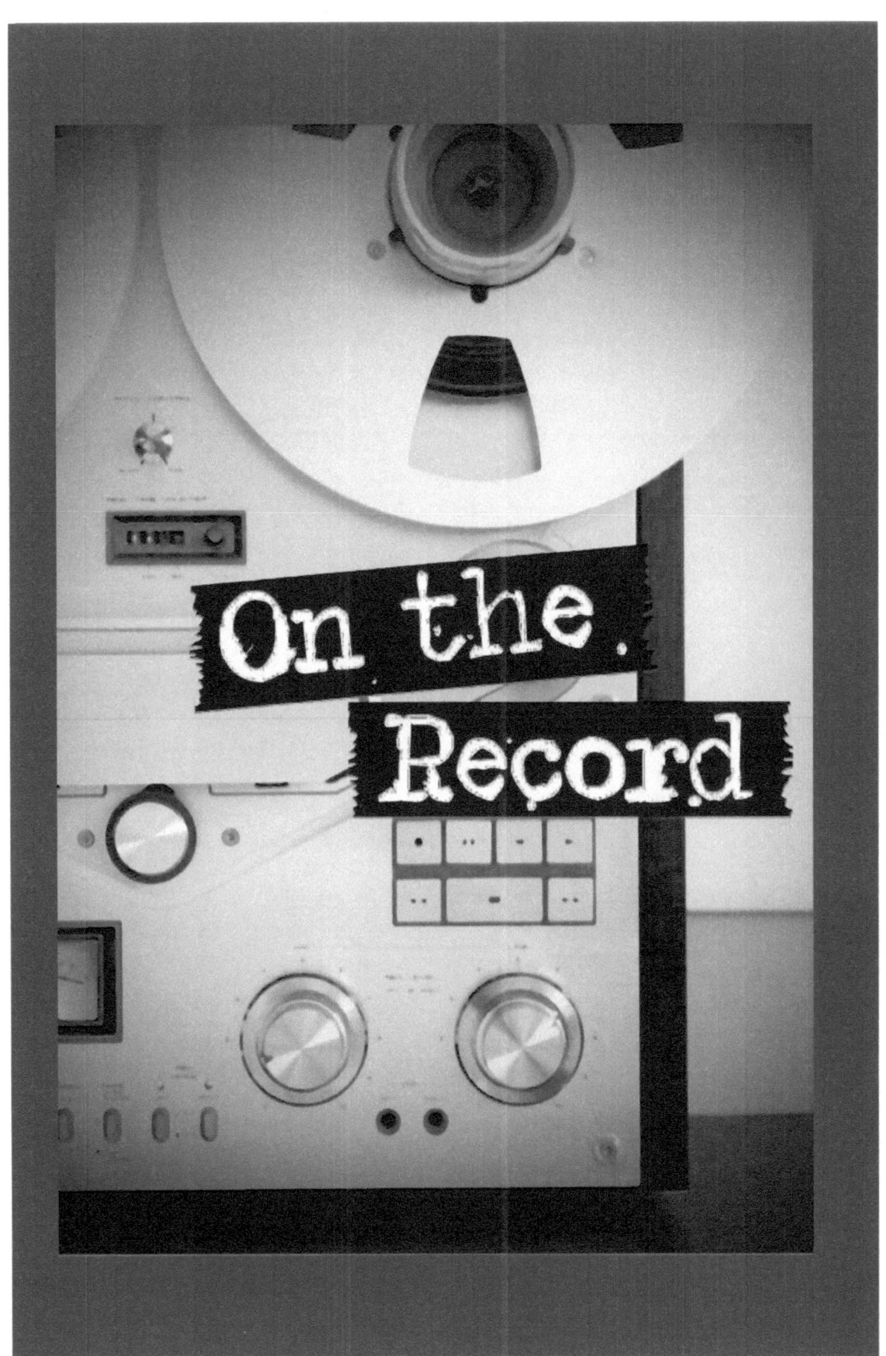
On the
Record

A Moment With Stuart Keane

So what is it like to be an author and cast your main character as an author themselves? Do you see yourself in Greg Irving?

In some ways, yes. The main inspiration for writing 89 was a simple one; the convention scene. I started attending conventions in 2015, when fellow author Matt Shaw invited me to London Film and Comic Con, and we've since found a common interest in doing them. So far, we've participated in four this year, and have several more on the 2016 schedule (see below for details). Attending various conventions is what planted the macabre seed for 89, and the idea just developed from there.

The convention scene and everything associated with the setup is the perfect setting for a horror story. Whilst attending, my brain put the finer details into place, and the story came about very quickly. My mind works in mysterious ways, but I also love to base my stories in reality. For me, sitting on a coach for a long journey and having someone sit right next to you, despite a hundred empty seats on the vehicle, is one of my pet hates. To avoid this, I will shy away from people, stick the headphones in, bury myself in my Kindle and get on with it. However, I also realised it was a great beginning for a tense, horrifying tale.

Greg was very much my avatar in this novella, many of his habits in the first few chapters – his schedule, work ethic, his rules, and his love for American diners – are all very similar to mine, and I very much injected a dose of myself into his character. It made writing him a lot of fun, and, for me, added some realism to the twisted plot. Writing what you know and love is always going to make a great story and I think it paid off; the feedback for 89 has been great, thus far. It was definitely an interesting writing process.

Sheffield hosts a lot of horror/sci-fi/thriller authors. Is there something about your city, region or otherwise that inspires this genre so widely?

I was born and raised in Kent, in a number of quaint villages and towns (Snodland, Tunbridge Wells, and Larkfield), but the county as a whole was very inspirational for me. As a kid, I grew up without the internet or the technology that is so easily accessible to today's youth, so my vivid imagination was my best friend for many years. I fondly remember long, beautiful summer days spent walking along the riverbank, and climbing into abandoned war shelters, navigating the local chalk quarries, reading amazing novels back-to-back under a tree, or even avoiding the local bullies with my friends; things that all children go through in their young adventures. At the time, it was my complete and utter world. You just go with it.

Those days are very much rooted in my brain, and everything I experienced, good or bad, was stored in a little memory lockbox. Slowly, these memories are emerging in my work, which makes the writing incredibly fun and memorable. Everyone likes to relive his or her childhood, but I get to do it for a living, which doesn't seem entirely fair. However, where I may stray into other worlds, or Lake Whisper (my go-to horror universe), I will always return to Kent, and portray my stories there. It has a certain inspiration I haven't found elsewhere.

There's something inspirational about using a real location; the place that provided the special background for your coming of age. A town where you've walked the cracked pavements, or scuffed your knees on the long grass, kissed one of the local girls, visited the sweet shop while the sun is ebbing away on the horizon, or smelt the burning bonfires that make you sniff and smile. I'll cherish these memories forever, but it means I can also find a sinister foil to match them, and thus turn them into an enjoyable horror story. It's a challenge I relish, and a great way to construct enjoyable stories.

You say that people have "enthralled" and "entertained" you with their "many, many adventures." Can you give us some examples of these and how they may have played out in influencing your writing?

As many of my readers know, Richard Laymon is the man who inspired me to write. I read Flesh when I was seven, and haven't looked back since. However, my horror education would soon expand and it wasn't long until I was consuming the works of Laymon and fellow horror authors Shaun Hutson, James Herbert, Clive Barker, and Stephen King. In later years, I would discover Richard Montanari, Robert Crais, Lee Child, Chris Carter, and Brett Battles as well. I enjoy thrillers as much as horror and I've always found that the two walk a very fine line, one that can segue into either genre at the drop of a hat.

These authors, and a number of others, are the combined reason I wanted to write. Yes, Laymon laid the initial groundwork for my curious, piqued interest, but the other authors all had a hand in it; King with Christine, a car that, to this day, still resonates with me fondly (my dream is to own my very own '58 Plymouth Fury). Barker with The Hellbound Heart, the first book to put goose flesh on my forearms, Hutson with his vivid, visceral style of writing, one that I find immensely fun to read, and Herbert with The Fog, the first horror book that I read twice. I met Lee Child for a meet and greet once, as the result of a writing contest prize, and he gave me the personal inspiration to follow my writing passion, so he had a helping hand in my career too.

All of these authors have helped pave the way for me. Many adventures from many hands, but the result is the same; hours of solid inspiration, books that encouraged me to pick up a pen and get creating. King himself says that if you don't read, you can't write. It's true, and this is concrete proof, a very honest truth in the world of fiction writing. They gave me their stories and adventures, and I remember how much fun I had escaping into their worlds for hours at a time. Those lazy days were incredible, and a lot of fun, which is why I aim to provide the same to others.

You wisely note that movies and books are two extremely different vehicles for storytelling. What is your favorite movie? Your favorite book? How are they different in the way they tell their story?

Wow, that's a hard question. I'm an avid film buff, so picking one movie is difficult. I would probably say The Godfather. It's pretty much the perfect movie. There's something special about a three-hour film that doesn't drag, one that scoops you up for the entire duration and carries you on a beautiful journey. The film is nearly perfect in every aspect. It's not a horror, but the urban suspense associated with such a gangster movie is very real, very gritty; you feel it in every scene and even on repeat viewing, you still wince a little when the violence hits. Any film that can do that to me is a winner in my book.

When it comes to books, it's just as difficult to select just one, so I'll go with a book I've read several times; Stephen King's It. Say what you will about horror's most famous author, King is one hell of a storyteller, and his tome about a mysterious entity in Derry was one of the scariest reads of my childhood. The first time I read it, over one long summer, was in 1993, at age twelve. A large section of the story involved a group of children in a small town – I was one myself at that point – so the book not only terrified me, but it also introduced me to the possibility that the world wasn't as harmless as it seemed. Society had a dark side, and this book opened my innocent eyes to that. To this day, it's a phenomenal read, and I highly recommend it to anyone who can stomach the 1,138 pages of terror within.

For films and books, there are many reasons the two mediums differ, but the main one is pure imagination. With a book, a story will play out one way in one mind, and completely differently in the next. It depends on the imagination as to where the story goes, what the characters look like, just how evil the big bad is, etc. With a film, the work is done for you; the details are served up on a plate. It can be liberating in cases, but I'm one of those people who prefers to imagine the scenario, not have it broadcast for me.

I personally think books are better than films for this reason, despite being a film buff, and any film based on a book falls into that category too. Jurassic Park was a phenomenal film, but the book was much better; darker, more foreboding, the sense of doom was almost electric. It's an experience you simply can't usher from a film unless you hit pay dirt with a rare cast and crew (I draw you again to the Godfather, the only book and movie combination that excels on both fronts), but with a book it can happen on every page. You just have to want it to.

What has been your favorite piece to write? Your least favorite?

To date, my favourite piece to write was Grin. The novel became a beast in its own right, and went to dark places I never expected to go. Dani – the 17-year-old main character – was a tour de force, one of the strongest, most conflicted characters I've ever committed to page, and not only did I enjoy writing her, I even changed her doomed fate – the only time I've ever done this. She was originally going to die, but I just couldn't pull the trigger. Now, six months later, I have three sequels planned. Thus far, she has been my most well received character, and the readers have all said how much they enjoyed her gruesome tale. I can say this; in 2017, you will see a lot more of Dani.

As it stands, I would say I enjoyed writing all of my stories – short story, novel or otherwise. I think if I wrote a story I didn't connect with, or enjoy, it would make the writing process very difficult and I doubt the story would end up completed. I know some authors who torture themselves with certain stories but luckily – touch wood – I haven't had that yet. It may happen though; like writer's block, I believe it's inevitable, and something every author experiences at least once.

What makes for a great setting for a story?

In my personal opinion, and this is a process I use regularly, I think a familiar setting is important to a story. Where have people been? What scares them? On the flipside of this, have I been there, do I know what it's like? Can I convey this into a story?

I like to write a scene and set it so the reader goes, 'Wait, I've been there before. Ugh.' Cue goose bumps and attention set. A serial killer is scarier when invading someone's living room or personal space than say, the moon. It's not always that simple, but if you can set the story in reality, and use a place people are very familiar with,

then the reader will relate to it. As a good example, a majority of one of my short stories, Wet, takes place in a bathtub. I've had several readers express their concern for the safety of that normal, mundane location since reading that dark tale. One even swore off bathing for life, but I hope she was joking. The storyfeatures in Whispers – Volume 1.

Setting the scene like that can be a very useful technique for a writer, and it's one I like to adhere to. As a reader, I like to be comfortable in my imaginary world, and being somewhere familiar is a great way to ensure that happens. My novels have all followed this process; locations include a cinema, a small town, a bustling city, a school, a coach; all places that a large selection of people have visited once or twice. If you can draw the reader in, it's a great way of keeping them hooked. I want people to enjoy my writing, so if I can make that happen by using the largest thing available to me, so be it.

What would you have told yourself 10 years ago about life as a writer? What do you want to tell your future self?

"The internet will be your best friend. It makes the writing and publishing process that much more accessible, friendly and interesting." If I had known this back then, and followed it up, I believe I would have been a lot further along in my writing career.

If I had to tell my future self something? "You did it, you achieved your dream."

Looks like you attended the Walker Stalker Con in London in early March. Do you go to many conventions? What has been your favorite?

As mentioned above, conventions are very much a part of my career now. I've attended four this year thus far, and still have several on the horizon. On the 2016 schedule thus far, I have Nottingham Em-Con (April 30th/May 1st), MCM Belgium (June 11th/12th), Sanitarium Horror Con (23rd July), Invicta Con (August 7th), and Bristol Horror Con (October 15th). There may be a few more added in due course.

I believe that paying it back to the readers – the very people who enable me to live my dream career – is very important. I enjoy mingling with my readers, having that personal side to me, one that authors rarely share, and hearing their feedback in person, well, it's definitely one of the better aspects of this career. I'm all for socializing with the readers in any way possible, and conventions are an excellent way to do this.

Of all the conventions so far, I would say Walker Stalker was definitely my favourite. Not only did I sell out by lunchtime on the Sunday, which was highly unexpected, but I also met some fantastic celebrities, a ton of amazing readers – many of whom have stayed in touch since – and really enjoyed myself. It was a true horror fans convention, and it opened my eyes to the dedication of the people who love the genre. The organiser's made you feel welcome too, at home, which is important for any guest or trader. I very much look forward to returning next year.

Do you ever hope your pieces are turned into feature-length films? How involved would you want to be in that process?

Funnily enough, All or Nothing is currently being worked into a screenplay for a potential TV serial. It's very early days, and I'm keeping my feet on the ground, but the process is very exciting nonetheless. The reason I looked into this avenue was simple; reader feedback, many of whom stated the format of All or Nothing would work perfectly in a miniseries. I'm lucky to have a few friends and screenwriters in the industry, so after a little negotiation, we made some headway. Fingers crossed it turns into something special.

As for feature film, I think every author dreams of seeing their work turned into a movie. It's like seeing your imagination ripped straight from your brain and realised in glorious colour and high definition. I can imagine that seeing your vision on a screen, with thousands of people watching, would be a true bucket list moment. I would like to remain involved in the process if this were to happen, but I think it's one of those rare moments where living it and dreaming it are two very different things. We'll see what the future holds. As an avid film buff, though, this would be a total dream come true.

Where do you hope to be as an author at the end of your life?

I hold onto the dream of a comfortable cabin in the woods, overlooking a shimmering lake, copses of trees on all sides, and watching the sun set while it illuminates the water with its glorious rays of dusk. And Christine parked in the driveway, ready to burn rubber at a moment's notice. For me, it's the perfect way to end my life, and career. Just my family, a comfortable home, my stories and my thoughts. Hopefully, that's many a decade away yet, but it's a beautiful thought, something to aspire to.

As we are hurtling through 2016, are there any works that you have come across that you highly recommend to horror readers?

I need to catch up on my reading, in all honesty. I'm currently revisiting the classics. I'm reading Battle Royale by Koushun Takami at present, and working on several horror novels that have become religious reading for me in recent years (It, The Stand, The Hellbound Heart). I have books on my shelf from Jack Rollins, Kyle M. Scott, Dave Basnett, Mark Parker, Matt Shaw, Iain Rob Wright, Matt Hickman, and a host of others, many of whom I consider the bright future of the horror genre. My reading pile isn't shrinking anytime soon; just the way I like it.

However, I also work for Dark Chapter Press, a promising publishing house from the UK, and I have to say this; some of thewriters I've discovered through various anthology submissions and competitions have been phenomenal. To name them all would take an entire page, but DCP prides itself in discovering and developing horror talent, and we have a whole host of them currently under our wing. Our most recent anthology, Kids, went to #1 in the UK and became a bestseller for its debut week. A second volume will be released in the summer, but if you want to see the future of horror, catch any release from Dark Chapter Press. Visit their website for more details: www.darkchapterpress.com

And, of course, I have a host of books in the pipeline. My next release will be The House That Hell Built, which was co-written with Matt Shaw and Michael Bray, and I am currently working on book 2 of the Charlotte Chronicles, Awakening. 8 Church Field, an urban home invasion horror, is also in the works, and I just finalized the first release of 2017. You can catch the details on my website, www.stuartkeane.com, or visit me on Facebook. I'm always networking on there.

Thank you for your time Stuart. If you want to find out a little more about Stuart or just want to pick up a few books, head over to his website:

http://www.stuartkeane.com/

So who is Stuart Keane?

Just an ordinary guy who likes to write thrilling, compelling stories. For thirty years, people have enthralled me, entertained me and provided me with many, many adventures. And inspiration. Now, I want to return the favour.

Hello horror lover.
If you've been suffering from a persistent desire
for just a little more unpleasantness in your life,
we have the answer:
NOCTURNAL
TRANSMISSIONS
PODCAST
Nocturnal Transmissions is a fortnightly podcast featuring
inspired performances of dark tales both old and new
by voice artist Kristin Holland.
Find them at
nocturnaltransmissions.com.au
or wherever good podcasts are purveyed.

If you have any feedback or would like to leave a review please head over to Amazon and share your thoughts about Sanitarium.

Thank you for your time and we salute your love for all things horror.

https://www.facebook.com/SanitariumPublishing

https://www.thesanitarium.co.uk/

https://twitter.com/sanitariumlit

https://www.instagram.com/sanitariumpublishing/